# CHARMED *by the* BARTENDER

## PIPER RAYNE

*Who knew sleeping with the enemy could be this fun?*

Was the one night stand a good idea?

Well, no. Probably not in retrospect.

In my defense I *had* just moved back into my grandparent's house, I'd lost my dream job, and a guy on Tinder had stood me up. It was like life had suddenly stamped 'LOSER' on my forehead.

So when the guy behind the bar started giving me THE look . . . you know, the one that promised I'd be screaming his name into the wee hours of the morning? When that guy also has the perfect amount of scruff on his chiseled chin, biceps bulging out of his t-shirt, and a cocky grin you knew he'd earned in the sack . . . when he gives you *that* look, you don't bother to figure out what your six degrees of separation are. You jump on that horse and ride it!

Pun fully and completely intended. And accurate by the way.

I fully admit to feeling sorry for myself and acting impulsively, but by the time I'd figured out WHO the bartender was, I was already falling for him.

# CHARMED
*by the*
# BARTENDER

Dedicated to all the ladies still
looking for their very own unicorn cock.

# chapter
## ONE

THIS IS THE START of an amazing new chapter in my life. At least that's what I keep reminding myself. How else will I get through today without curling up into a ball in my bed and feeling like the world's biggest loser?

I reach my friend Tahlia's apartment door and knock. Seconds later the door is whipped open and there stands one of my oldest, prettiest, richest friends. But I love her despite her perfect life.

She smiles wide and her blue eyes sparkle. "I'm so happy you're home," Tahlia says as she envelops me in a hug before dragging me through the door. She still smells like the expensive perfume she's worn since high school.

"Me, too." For the most part, that's true. Returning to San Francisco, the city I grew up in, is a welcome change. I never quite made the same connections in Sacramento that I had with the girls I'd known since junior high.

Returning to the house I was raised in, which also happens to house two seventy-somethings? Not so stellar. But beggars can't be choosers, as they say, and I was one bad decision away from being penniless and selling my body on a street corner.

"Ah! Is that Whit?" Lennon screams from the living room. Before I can blink she's bounding down the hallway toward me, her cropped near-black hair bouncing as she does, the tattoos covering her arms a blur as she flails her limbs around like she's preparing for take-off.

"You look like an interpretive dancer on crack," I say with a laugh as she barrels into me.

She squeezes me tight and then pulls away. "Really?" She turns the corners of her mouth down. "I've been trying so hard to lay off the crack. I'm pretty much just sticking to meth now."

I roll my eyes at the most outgoing and insane of my two best friends.

Some things you need to know about Lennon are that she's rarely serious, is always pushing you out of your comfort zone, and prides herself on being able to tie a cherry stem with her tongue in ten seconds flat. Enough said.

"Someone who didn't know you might just believe you," Tahlia says as she pulls her blonde hair back into a ponytail with an elastic she has around her wrist. She's still wearing her suit so she must've just gotten home from work at her father's company.

Must be nice. The work part, I mean, not the working for her father part, because that man could be Tony Soprano's half-brother, minus the Mob. At least I think so.

"Like I'd care," Lennon mumbles as she heads back the way she came.

"I'm going to change out of this outfit," Tahlia says. "Head on in and pour yourself a glass of wine. I stopped and picked up some appetizers for us. They're laid out on the table in the living room."

"Awesome. I could use something to dull the edges of the fact that I moved back into my grandparents' house this afternoon."

She gives me a sympathetic head tilt and rubs my back before we start down the hall. "It's only temporary, Whit. You'll be on your feet again in no time."

"Or on your knees. If you're lucky," Lennon calls out.

We're both laughing as Tahlia turns right to head to her bedroom and I move the opposite direction in search of the alcohol.

Her condo isn't huge, but it's modern and sleek and I'm sure must cost her more than I made in a month, since it's in downtown San Francisco. Glass walls showcase the city lights beneath us and, coupled with the open-concept design of the kitchen, living, and dining room areas, the space feels airy and light.

Lennon and I catch up for a few minutes while we wait for Tahlia to rejoin us. As usual, her antics equally make me laugh and cringe. We all went to college in the Bay area and kept in touch through college. After college I left town to take a job at the local Sacramento newspaper, but there's something comforting about knowing I'll be seeing them on the regular now that I've returned to my hometown. We're back to being the three amigos, as unlikely as our group is, given our differing personalities.

Tahlia enters the kitchen with a strange expression on her face. I've known her long enough to see that she's trying to suppress a grin. There's something she's keeping from us. With anyone else I'd start prying, but she's like an overstuffed vault filled with confetti. If we give her enough time she won't be able to stand it and it will all come bursting out.

After she's poured herself a glass of wine the three of us head into her living room, where Lennon makes herself comfortable on Tahlia's brown leather chair while Tahl and I opt to sit on the cream suede couch.

A small tray of pristine-looking appetizers sits on the circular coffee table accompanied by small plates and napkins. I honestly don't know why Tahlia wastes her talents at her father's company. She'd be an amazing event planner. I know her mother drilled into her the importance of entertaining properly since birth, but she has a natural knack for making everyone around her comfortable and creating a memorable experience when you're in her care.

"Any luck on the job front?" she asks before setting her wine glass down on the table with an exaggerated flourish.

"Nothing yet. I plan on applying for anything and everything I'm qualified for tomorrow, though."

"If you're really stuck I know a guy who might be looking for someone," Lennon says as she shoves one of the appetizers into her mouth. "I can't promise it would all be entirely legal, but—"

"I think I'll pass," I respond with a laugh and take a healthy sip from my wine glass.

Lennon studies me for a second. "Yeah, I don't think you could pull off a prison jumpsuit. Orange isn't your color. Me, on the other hand . . . I could rock that baby like I was on the set of *Orange Is the New Black.*"

All three of us break out in laughter at her reference since she's constantly told that she looks like one of the characters from that show. I swear I don't see it, so it must be that she's used her body as a canvas for her tattoos.

Tahlia presses her hands to her chest while she laughs and I'm practically blinded by the glare of a giant diamond on her ring finger. Of her left fucking hand.

Lennon must notice at the same time because she spits half her wine out all over herself. "Holy hell, Tahl. What the fuck?"

A huge grin spreads across Tahlia's face and she lets out a squeal like she's thirteen years old and just found out that One Direction just got back together. "I'm engaged! Chase asked me last night!"

We all scream and flap our arms in unison, doing a really good imitation of Lennon's earlier crackhead impersonation. We pop up off of Tahl's expensive furniture and embrace in an awkward three-person hug. I'm understanding now why in most threesomes two people do all the work on the other one. Trying to spread the love out evenly between three people is pretty impossible.

At least that's what people who watch porn tell me.

Anyway, moving on.

Lennon and I inspect the huge hunk of rock on Tahl's finger. It's so big that I'm sure she's going to end up having one massive bicep on her left arm and she'll be reduced to wearing long-sleeve shirts even in the summer months just to hide it.

"This is absolutely beautiful," I say, moving her hand back and forth so the diamond catches the light. "How did he propose?"

"Chase took me to our favorite restaurant and had the waiter place it on top of my dessert. He got down on one knee in front of the entire restaurant. Everyone started clapping and cheering." Her smile is huge and lights up her entire face.

My initial thought is that Chase's proposal was a little cliché and unimaginative, but my friend is happy, so who am I to judge?

"Have you told your parents?" Lennon asks as we all sit back down.

Tahlia nods. "I called them last night. They're thrilled. Obviously." A small blush creeps into her cheeks.

Tahl's parents would be thrilled. She's going to be marrying into the Webber family—one of San Francisco's most prominent families with high-society lineage. Even those of us who don't travel in those circles know about the Webbers. I'm sure Tahl's mom's vision for her life is complete now that she's marrying well.

"I'm so excited for you! Do you know when you'll have

the wedding?" I lean forward and grab my wine glass back off the table.

Tahlia shakes her head. "Not yet."

"Well, that's one off the market. More for me," Lennon jokes.

"You're going to have so much fun planning this wedding," I say then take a sip of my wine.

"As long as I can get my mother off my back. I'm sure she's going to want to employ some high-priced wedding planner so she can make sure all *her* ideas are made into a reality. Whatever though." She waves her hand in front of her. "I'll figure it out."

*Good luck with that,* I think but don't say.

"So, Lennon, what's up with you?" Tahlia asks. "Why did you want to get together tonight?"

Lennon mocks insult. "Can't a girl just want to hang out with her two best friends in the world?"

"Not really. Not you. You made it sound so formal," I say.

She fidgets in her seat and I realize that she's nervous. Which is so not at all like her. Something is definitely up.

"There was something I wanted to talk to you both about."

Tahlia and I both lean forward in our seats, anxious to hear what she has to say, but she's silent. Finally, Tahl says, "And that would be . . ."

"Well, I guess I should start at the beginning." She tips her wine glass back and takes a couple of big gulps before setting it down on the table. "You know how everyone, especially my brother, is always telling me to get serious and figure out what I want to do with my life, right?"

We both nod because, yeah. Lennon's been told that more than a few times by her family.

"Usually I just tune that shit out. It's kinda like that teacher on Charlie Brown. All I hear is muh-muh-muh. But about six months ago, I was chatting with this girl named Carly and she'd been through so much—homelessness, addiction, not graduating high school. But she was still so motivated and had such a vision for her life that it sort of made me feel guilty for not appreciating how easy I've had it in comparison."

I almost feel as if I don't know this girl in front of me. She looks like Lennon. She talks like Lennon. But Lennon is almost never serious like this.

"Where did you meet this girl?" I ask, curious.

"I met her at an AA meeting." Lennon's eyes flare for a second and she brings her hand to her mouth. "Shit. I don't think I'm supposed to say that."

I don't respond to that comment because I'm still wondering what the hell she was doing at an AA meeting. "What the hell were you doing at an AA meeting?" Tahlia says. It's like she can read my mind.

Lennon shrugs. "I was bored one night and I passed by a sign outside a church that said there was a meeting going on. I was curious so I went in."

"You just went into an AA meeting even though you're not an alcoholic?" I ask, just to be sure I heard her right.

"Pretty much." She reaches forward and grabs one of the appetizers from the tray and places it on the plate in front of her. "Why, are you not supposed to do that?" She looks genuinely confused.

"I'm pretty sure you're not," Tahlia responds in a serious voice.

Lennon just shrugs it off again. "It was more boring than I thought it would be. No one really shared any crazy stories or anything." She looks off into the distance like she's deep in thought. "Shame really. I thought for sure when I sat beside the guy with all the neck tattoos and feather boa that he'd have some sordid tales to tell."

"Lennon, you tattoo people for a living and have tattoos

everywhere yourself." I bring the wine to my lips and take a small sip.

"It doesn't mean I can't judge other people who have them."

Both Tahlia and I give each other a look and then roll our eyes.

"You were saying," Tahl says in an attempt to get Lennon back on track.

"Oh, right. Well, we got into this long conversation about how her life was in the shitter five years ago, and how she clawed her way out. No one thought she could do it but she persevered and now she's a very successful business owner."

"Don't you enjoy tattooing people anymore?" I ask because I can't imagine Lennon in a business suit. She's . . . artsy. She always has been. Lennon is at her best when she's able to express herself creatively.

"You know me, I love adhering permanent art to other people's bodies, but I don't know. Lately, I've felt like I need more, you know?"

Tahl and I nod our heads and I think I'm able to hide my surprise. I love my friend, but I honestly didn't realize she ever thought about anything beyond the moment.

"It got me thinking," Lennon carries on. "What am I good at? What am I interested in?"

"Dudes with beards?" Tahlia guesses.

"Not showering on Sundays?" I say.

"Making people uncomfortable?"

"Dining and dashing?"

"Oh, I know," Tahlia says, waving her hand in the air. "Our old high school teacher Mr. Butler."

"You guys are hilarious," Lennon deadpans.

Tahlia and I laugh. "All right. All right. What is it?" I ask.

"Art! And sex!"

Hmm. I guess we missed the obvious.

"No argument there," Tahlia says.

Lennon takes a deep breath and if I didn't know her better, I might think that she's actually nervous about whatever she's about to tell us.

"I want to start a sex toy company."

Both Tahlia and I sit there in silence and stare at her for a full minute.

"A sex toy company?" I ask, making sure I heard her right.

Lennon nods with a big grin on her face. "Yep. Most women are so sexually repressed it's ridiculous." She cuts a look over to Tahlia, but doesn't comment further. "Why is it okay for men to be sexual and enjoy sex but for some reason it's taboo for us?"

"I don't know," I respond honestly.

"I want to create a line that's artsy and sleek. Devices that any woman would be proud to have—ones she doesn't feel obligated to hide in her nightstand, mortified at the thought of someone finding them. I want my customer to be a woman proud of her sexuality."

She hops up off the leather chair and scurries across to the kitchen, grabbing her large tote off the counter and bringing it back to the living room with her. When she takes her seat again she's sitting cross-legged as she rummages through her purse.

Tahlia has been pretty quiet and I wonder what she's thinking given that she's the businesswoman out of all of us.

"I want you two to be my guinea pigs. I need honest opinions about the product. Look, feel . . . performance." Lennon glances up at us and waggles her eyebrows.

I chuckle.

"I call these vibrators Tickled Pink." She reaches into her bag and pulls out two hot pink, phallic-shaped sex toys wrapped in plastic. "The Tickled Pink vibrators are completely waterproof, made of a soft outer shell that's designed to feel like the real thing, and you can wash them with soap and water." She stands to deliver one to both Tahl and me. "I've already loaded them up with batteries so you're good to get off."

Lennon takes her seat again and looks at us expectantly.

"What do you expect us to do with these?" Tahlia asks, looking a little mortified.

"Use them." Lennon rolls her eyes.

I pull mine from the plastic packaging and give it the once-over. I have to admit, it is attractive as far as these things go. It's sleek and modern-looking. I'm no expert, but it doesn't look anything like the scary, veiny, monster cock contraptions that come to mind when I think of vibrators.

"It's cute," I say.

"Thanks." Lennon sits up a little higher in her chair, seeming to enjoy the fact that I've complimented her product.

"How were you able to get this made?" Tahlia asks, ever the businesswoman. "It can't have been cheap."

Lennon shrugs. "I used some of the money from my grand-parents' inheritance to fund it. I need to make sure my products are on point before I go hunting for investors to launch the line."

"You're going to blow your whole inheritance on this?" Tahlia gestures to the vibrator in her hand. "I thought that was supposed to be to purchase a house?"

A flash of hurt crosses over Lennon's face, but she schools her features quickly. I know Tahl doesn't mean anything by it, that she's just looking out for her friend, but I feel bad for Lennon. "Well, if this takes off, I'll have even more money to purchase a house in the end, won't I?"

Tahlia and Lennon hold one another's gaze for a moment before I interject.

"If anyone can do it you can, Lennon. I know you'll find your investor and get this thing off the ground."

She sends a grateful smile my way.

"If you need any help with a business plan or anything let

me know," Tahl says.

Lennon directs her smile her way and I know that the brief moment of tension is behind us.

The three of us catch up for a while longer before Lennon rises from the chair. "It's been swell, ladies, but I have a date to put some D in the P." She makes a circle with her thumb and index finger on her left hand and inserts the pointer finger of her right hand through it over and over. "Catch you on the flip side."

"I didn't know you were dating anyone," I say.

She looks over her shoulder at me as she bends to pick up her purse off the floor. The crinkle in her forehead tells me she's either confused or thinks I'm an idiot. "I'm not dating. Didn't you hear what I just said? I'm off to get laid. Totally different."

Sometimes I envy her. Lennon never seems to let pesky things like responsibility, morals, or society's standards weigh her down. She's a free bird who does what she wants when she wants.

I, on the other hand, am borderline-obsessed with making something of myself. Which makes the fact that I was laid off from my last job even worse.

The childhood therapist my grandparents made me see said my overzealous drive was because my mother had pawned me off on her parents when I was just an infant and never showed her face again. That coupled with the fact that I'd never known my father apparently meant that I was subconsciously trying to prove myself worthy of love.

What did she know? Ten years of school and a black leather couch in your office did not an expert make.

I just value security and I want to be able to support myself. No sense relying on someone else when all they'll do is let you down.

"I should get going, too," I say.

Tahlia does this thing with her face where the corners of her lips both angle down and she looks like a Snapchat filter gone wrong. "Are you sure you can't stay longer?"

"I live here now, remember? We can see each other all the time now. Besides, after your big news, I'm sure you're anxious to spend the rest of the night with Chase." I waggle my eyebrows and Tahl breaks out in a grin.

"Whit is right. Go spend the night between the sheets reminding that boy why he put a ring on it," Lennon says before turning to strut down the hall.

Tahlia rolls her eyes and then follows us to her door to say her goodbyes. Ever the good hostess.

"Chase's parents would like to have an engagement party at some point in the next couple of weeks. I can count on you girls to be there, right?"

I lean in and hug her and then Lennon follows suit. "Of course you can," I say.

"I wouldn't miss the opportunity to watch your mother's eyes roll back into her head when she sees me," Lennon adds.

Tahl laughs as the two of us make our exit.

Tahlia's mother has never really liked Lennon. She's much too colorful for the Santoras. If I'm honest, I've only ever had the impression that Mrs. Santora tolerates me. Like Lennon, I didn't come from oodles of money (obviously), but unlike Lennon, my skin isn't a canvas for self-expression, and so I'm better able to hide that fact.

When Lennon steps out into the hallway she spins around and calls out, "Ladies, don't forget to put your Tickled Pink vibrator to the test. I'm expecting a report back!"

An older couple passing by in the hallway give her a horrified look and scamper off as fast as their elderly legs will take them and we all break out into hysterics.

I wave back at Tahlia and loop my arm through Lennon's and we walk down the hall toward the elevator. "It's good to be home," I say.

When we step out onto the street we walk for a second along the sidewalk before she stops beside a van parked on the side of the street. It's then that I notice the VW van she's driven since college is wrapped in a design of cartoon unicorns, some of which are shitting and throwing up rainbows. I raise an eyebrow.

Lennon looks from me to the vehicle and back again. "What? I like unicorns."

"Okaaaaaay . . . do you think maybe this is taking it a little too far?"

She shrugs. "Lester needed a paint job and it was cheaper to have it wrapped. I could have gone with something boring, but where's the fun in that?"

Such a Lennon answer. I roll my eyes and begin walking away.

"Hey, what are you doing? Hop in." She gestures to the bright monstrosity beside her.

"I'm going to walk."

"Don't be silly. I'll drop you wherever it is you want to go."

I shake my head. "I can get myself home. You go have fun with Mr. Right Now."

She angles a hip and crosses her arms in front of her chest. "I know you *can* get yourself home on your own, but you don't have to."

We stand, staring at each other for a moment, before she continues.

"I realize you hate relying on anyone for anything, Whit, but not everything is an imposition. Not everyone is going to let you down." When I pin her with a stare, she raises her hands in a placating gesture. "Just sayin'."

And that's how I find myself driving through the hilly streets of San Francisco, Lil Wayne blasting from the speakers, inside a giant fucking unicorn.

# chapter
## TWO

*T*HE NEXT NIGHT I wander around the city wallowing and lamenting my current predicament. I finally decide on a small bar named the Thirsty Monk, in the Nob Hill section of the city. The place is cute with small round tables throughout and a long U-shaped bar in the middle of the space. I take a seat at said bar and chat off and on with the female bartender as she feeds me a steady supply of drinks.

The longer I sit here, the more it dawns on me that I'm twenty-five, unemployed, and living with my grandparents. I've never felt like a bigger loser in my life. The rotting cherry on top of this shit cream sundae is that Tahlia is getting married.

Don't get me wrong, I'm ecstatic for my friend. I really am. But I know that the coming months are going to be filled with parties, wedding rites of passage, and all that other stuff. Which if I wasn't at the lowest point in my life I'd have a lot more enthusiasm for. Plus, the small voice inside willing me to acknowledge the truth knows that I'm feeling sorry for myself. Why can't *I* have all those things?

When we were younger we had dreams of all of us getting

married around the same time and starting our families together. Girlish dreams, I know, but the disappointment over the fact that it will never be is just shy of crushing. Tahlia is moving on with her life and I'm just . . . stuck.

Back when we were still teenagers with stars in our eyes, we'd decided that I'd be Tahlia's maid of honor, Tahlia would be Lennon's, and Lennon would be mine. It seemed the easiest way to avoid an argument down the line. That, and we'd watched that episode of *Friends* where Monica, Rachel, and Phoebe did the same thing. Okay, maybe we were just being copycats.

Being Tahlia's maid of honor is not going to be an inexpensive venture and at the moment I barely have enough to buy myself dinner at Taco Bell. I need to get a job and quick.

About an hour after that realization I'm checking my email on my phone in case any of the places I applied to earlier have responded and the Tinder app catches my eye.

Maybe it's the alcohol, maybe it's the dumpster that is my life, but getting laid by a stranger without the pretense of either of us wanting more seems like a fantastic idea right now.

And so I start swiping. And swiping.

Eventually one of the more attractive guys I swiped right on messages me a picture of his dick.

How's that for hello?

Judging by the picture though, he's working with some good equipment.

Never let it be said that a dick pic can't bring two people together.

Seconds later another message comes through.

*Pussylickr69: Wanna fuck?*

Well. He certainly doesn't waste time on pleasantries, does he? Ignoring the fact that this douche couldn't be bothered to even say hello or ask my name before asking if I wanted to bump uglies with him, I respond because in truth, tonight I only need what genetics has so clearly blessed him with.

> *Whiteebanter: That's the idea.*

> *Pussylickr69: Awesome. Where r u?*

> *Whiteebanter: At the Thirsty Monk in Nob Hill.*

> *Pussylickr69: Why don't u cum 2 my place?*

Since this is my first ever hook-up of this sort I don't know if it's normal to head over to the other person's place, but there isn't a chance in hell I'm going inside some stranger's house without meeting him in public and seeing if I get the creep vibe from him first. I have a very healthy creep-o-meter.

> *Whiteebanter: This is my 1$^{st}$ time doing this. Why don't you meet me here & we can have a drink then head to your place?*

I toss back the last of my drink while I wait for a response. Somehow the thirty seconds feels longer than it did waiting for the next season of *Breaking Bad* to air. Finally, his response comes.

> *Pussylickr69: Be there in 20.*

I drop my phone back into my purse hanging from the corner of the chair with the flair of a woman who's just taken ownership over her life.

Okay, I'm doing this. I'm really doing this.

I need another jolt of liquid courage before this guy shows up. I look up to order another drink expecting to see the pretty blonde who's been serving me all night, but instead my eyes meet a set of hazel eyes fringed with dark lashes. Those eyes are set in the face of a guy whose bone structure would make any model jealous. Further inspection tells me that his body is no less impressive. Muscles bulge beneath his taut t-shirt, the hard planes of his chest and abs clearly visible beneath. My gaze darts back up to his face to see a half-crooked smile and a gleam in his eyes that tells me he knows how hot he is.

After some work to reconnect my brain synapses with my tongue I'm finally able to speak.

"Hey. You don't look like the last bartender," I say and push my empty glass toward him.

"You're right. She's much cuter than I am."

His grin widens. And oh! There's a dimple, too. I've always been a sucker for a guy with a dimple. Then again, who isn't? I think of dimples as being the key to the chastity belt.

"Ready for a refill?" He nods down to the empty glass.

When I remember that a stranger is on his way to meet me so we can have sex together, panic flares inside me. I desperately need that drink.

"Yes!" I say with too much enthusiasm.

He doesn't comment on my over-excited nature, thankfully. "What'll you have?"

I ponder for a moment, thinking that I need something stronger than what I've been drinking—I'm going to need to be buzzed for this—but unsure what to order. "Something that will put hair on my chest," is my brilliant response to his question.

His gaze darts down to my cleavage. "Now why would you want to go and ruin a perfectly good chest like that?" He arches a brow, but instead of waiting for me to reply, he turns and begins to make my drink.

My face heats and a small portion of the confidence I've lacked lately returns. I smile to myself as he grabs a glass and adds ice to it, enjoying the way the muscles in his arms contract and relax as he sets about his work.

I'm so lost in ogling his body that I barely notice when he sets a drink in front of me.

"For the lady," he says in that deep, slightly raspy voice.

"Thank you." I lean forward and draw the drink up the

straw, not missing the way he's watching my lips with intense focus. The sweetness of the cola hits my tongue first and then the taste of whiskey followed by something else I can't place. "This is really good. What's it called?"

"A Stiffy." One corner of his lip tips up in a grin.

"What's in it?" I ask as I lean in for another sip. I've never been a huge whiskey drinker, but this stuff goes down smooth.

"It's my own creation." He winks and leans over the bar so close to me that his lips are practically touching my ear. "If I told you there's no telling the things I'd have to do to you to keep you quiet."

A shiver runs up my spine and he must notice because he chuckles as he backs away, amusement lighting his eyes.

"What's your name?" he asks.

"Whitney Knight. Most of my good friends call me Whit, though."

He places both palms on the bar top and lets his weight transfer to them, causing all the muscles to bunch up. Not that I notice because that would be slutty since I have another guy on his way here to screw my brains out.

The scent of his cologne wafts my way as he leans in just a little. "I hope I have the pleasure of being able to call you Whit someday then."

I swallow hard, my tongue feeling heavy in my mouth. "What's your name?" I ask in a breathy voice that probably gives away how turned on I am at that moment.

"Cole," he says simply.

Cole. Just one look at this guy and I know he's trouble. What I can't be sure of yet is whether he's more trouble than he's worth.

# chapter
# THREE

**A**N HOUR AND A half later and hot stuff has come around the bar to take the seat beside me and join me on my mission to get shit-faced. I have to admit, I'm enjoying his company, but it doesn't exactly make him Employee of the Year given the fact that he's supposed to be working.

"Won't your boss be mad that you're drinking on the job?" I ask.

That damn dimple makes another appearance again before he answers. "Nah, he's cool. It's dead in here tonight. If anyone comes in, I'll be sure they get what they need." His gaze rakes up and down my small frame, and I get the distinct impression that he's picturing me naked.

Jeez, I hope my nakedness looks amazing in his brain. Given the half-crooked smile on his face, I think it must. I wonder if his imagination is good enough to picture that dimple in my ass that doesn't ever seem to want to disappear, regardless of how much I weigh.

As if he's tempted fate with his words, the bell over the door dings and an older gentleman walks in and seats himself at one of the bar tables across the room.

"Be right back." Cole pats my hand before he rises from his seat.

It was an innocent gesture, but it makes me think dirty things. The heat from his hand seeps up my arm like a bee sting and settles somewhere in my chest.

I watch him walk away and can't help but notice the way his ass perfectly fills out his jeans. It bunches and flexes as his long strides take him across the bar. Maybe Lennon is right and it *has* been too long since I've been with a man.

It's then that I realize that Tinder dude still hasn't shown up. The bar isn't busy, probably since it's the middle of the week, and I've been chatting—okay, flirting—with Cole and hadn't realized how much time had passed. I grab my phone from my purse and open the app to see that I have a new message.

> *Pussylickr69: Not coming. Sorry found someone else who wasn't so much werk.*

Fury causes my face to heat as I type out a quick reply that might be, and by that I mean most definitely is, alcohol-fueled.

> *Whiteebanter: Yeah, I can see how thirty minutes of conversation is too much foreplay for you. Fuck you and your lack of knowledge of the English language. You spell work with an 'o,' dipshit.*

There. That'll show him. With a frown, I drop my phone back into my purse.

"Everything okay?" Cole asks as he takes the seat beside me again.

I sigh. "Yeah, I just found out that Pussylicker isn't coming anymore."

Cole nearly spits out the sip of drink he's just taken and has a coughing fit before he fully recovers. "Excuse me?"

"I was waiting for a guy from Tinder to show up, but he just ditched me because apparently it was too much work to have a drink with me before taking me back to his place to bang me." I spin my glass in place on the bar top.

"You're trolling for guys on Tinder?" Cole howls with laughter so hard he has to hold his stomach. I love the way the laugh looks on his face—the way it crinkles his eyes at the corners and how it showcases his perfect teeth. But all that aside, it's irritating.

"It's not that funny." This guy might be hot, but right now he's working my nerves.

"Actually, it is. Why the hell would a woman like *you* resort to finding someone to fuck on a dating site?"

The way the word 'fuck' rolls off his tongue has all my womanly parts contracting and wishing that it was an invitation to do just that. But never mind that, because I'm annoyed at him, I just barely remember through my drunken haze.

"What do you mean a *woman like me*?" I try to do air quotes around the last part, but my balance isn't what it was three hours ago, and I almost topple off my stool, so I quickly grab on to the bar in front of me.

"Beautiful. Intelligent. Likable. Smartass." He ticks each word off on one hand while he speaks and he says it like he means it. I hold his stare for a minute before realization dawns.

"Hey! I'm a B.I.L.F. You know, like a M.I.L.F. Only different." I'm so impressed that I thought of that given my current state.

Cole chuckles with an amused gleam in his eyes. "Only better," he says.

Our gazes lock for a beat and it's at that moment I know that if I offer myself up to this guy, he'll be more than willing to send me on the walk of shame tomorrow morning. Heat rushes into my cheeks and I look away. As much bravado as I had earlier about my Tinder escapade, I'm not sure I can do this. Be this girl so full of confidence that she bangs a stranger with no qualms about it.

My elation has crash-landed on the ground as I realize I'm not able to pull the trigger and make an advance toward him. I also know I'll probably regret it forever because this man is so far beyond good-looking that it's a speck in the rear-view mirror. Not to mention the fact that he's sexy as hell and seems to be a decent human being. Which is more impossible to find in the Bay area than someone who doesn't think they're allergic to gluten.

I take a deep breath and finish the last couple of gulps of my drink and push the glass in Cole's direction.

"Another, please."

Cole tosses back the rest of his drink and I watch as his Adam's apple bobs in his throat while the liquid slides down.

Damn. That is sexy.

*Why* is that sexy?

"I'm going to join you for another as well." He gets up off his bar stool and before walking away he comes to stand directly behind me. "Assuming you want me to stick around?"

His breath washes across my neck and my ear and I close my eyes for a brief moment to enjoy the sensation. "I'd like that," I say with all honesty.

"Good. I know the first guy let you down, but don't worry . . . I've been told I lick pussy like a boss."

And with that, he walks away while I struggle to keep my heart from pounding out of my chest.

I'm out of my league with this guy. I know it and there's a good chance that he knows it, too.

But ask yourself this, ladies . . . if you were called up to the big leagues from the minors, would *you* say no?

# chapter
# FOUR

*I* THINK I'M DEAD.

Wait. Would I be in this much pain if I were dead?

Probably not.

Maybe I'm just dying.

I scrunch my eyes closed in an effort to dull the roaring pain that unleashes itself inside my skull every time I move.

I'm serious. I just twitched my big toe and it felt like a knife driving into my brain.

It takes a minute, but I register that I must be in bed. I can feel the pillow under my head, the blankets bunched around my waist. I try to remember the last thing I was doing before waking with what feels like a ten-pound weight on my head. I feel like I'm Wile E Coyote and the Roadrunner just dropped the safe on me.

After what could be a few minutes, or maybe an hour—I'm really not sure—I brave opening my eyes. Slowly my eyelids peel apart and thank God for small favors . . . I'm not met with blazing sunlight to my retinas.

But I have no idea where the hell I am.

I'm in a bedroom. That much I can tell. A clean and sparse bedroom. Hardwood floors that look to be original, but redone, fill the room and white sheets cover me in a big bed. Dark curtains have been pulled over the set of large windows on the far side of the room so that they let in a small amount of light and a worn dresser sits at the far end of the bed.

I attempt to sit up to investigate further, but my head revolts and so I set it back down on the pillow. As I roll to the side I will my mind to remember what the hell I was doing last night.

I spot a bottle of water and two Advil on the night table and it's like seeing a mirage in the middle of the desert, I'm that thankful. That feeling is short-lived when I notice a note beside them.

Because that's when the night before comes rushing back to me. Feeling sorry for myself. The Tinder douchebag standing me up. Flirting with the bartender . . .

Reluctantly I raise my head, slowly so as not to cause my brain matter to leak out of my ears. What kind of house guest would I be then? There's enough light in the room that I'm able to read the masculine scrawl.

*I have to assume that after last night you need these. Sorry I had to leave, but I had an early appointment this morning. Stay as long as you like, but be sure to leave your number for me. Don't worry about locking up. The door will lock automatically behind you.*

*Cole*

*PS~ Can I call you Whit now? Since you're waking up half-naked in my bed I assume you consider us 'friendly.'*

Oh. My. God.

Oh, my God!

I rack my brain for any memory of what happened last night, but I can't even remember leaving the bar with him.

I'm still wearing my bra and underwear so I can't imagine we had sex then, right? I shift my pelvis around a bit. It doesn't feel like I had sex.

I bring my hands up to my face and groan.

I have no idea whether or not I had sex last night. As far as things go, this situation isn't doing a whole lot to raise my level of self-esteem.

Not to mention the fact that if I did have sex with him I really would have liked to remember it. There's a good chance I won't ever have a man like that between my legs again. Not because I don't think I'm worth it, but because sexual fantasies like Cole who aren't completely full of themselves aren't exactly an abundant commodity.

Unable to take the jackhammering in my head any longer, I sit up and reach for the Advil and water. Once I've swallowed the pills I set the glass back down on the bedside table and notice a pen there. That must be how he expects me to leave my number.

Not a chance in hell.

My phone rests on the nightstand, too, so I pick it up and bring up Lennon's contact info. If anyone is an expert at the one-night stand, it's her. It takes a few rings, but she eventually answers.

"This better be good. My date from last night was just about to chow down."

"Oh, sorry. Are you out for breakfast?"

Lennon laughs. "Sweet, innocent Whitney. I meant on my pussy."

I don't even know what to say to that so I ignore it entirely. "I just woke up in a stranger's bed, he's gone and left me a note, and I have no idea what happened between us last night."

I hear her cover the phone, some muffled talking on her part, and then she rejoins our conversation. "Tell me everything!"

"As long as you promise not to talk so loud, my hangover is in full effect."

"You were drunk last night?" she asks.

"Based on the hangover I'm currently experiencing and the fact that I remember jack shit about last night, I must have ended up *really* drunk."

"Uh-oh."

"Exactly."

My friends and a couple of my exes have filled me in on what I'm like when I'm really drunk. Let's just say that I'm amorous. To an extreme. I love my friends. I love everybody.

"I guarantee you that you were handsy," Lennon says and then laughs at my expense.

I can only imagine what I would have been like around someone as fuckable as Cole. The last thing I'm going to do is sign myself up for the embarrassment of seeing him again. No, thank you.

"I know, I know. Listen. What's the protocol here?" I ask. I roll myself out of bed (and I mean that literally) and find the bathroom just outside the door to his bedroom.

"What do you mean?"

"He left me a note and he wants my number."

"Okaaay . . . so what's the problem?"

I do my business quickly while holding the phone in the crook of my neck.

"The problem is that I'm mortified. I have no idea what happened last night and what I might have said." I glance at myself while I'm washing my hands. "I just saw myself in the mirror. I am such a hot mess right now."

Make-up is smeared down my face and I have dark circles under my eyes. My pallor is that of a corpse that's been rotting for a few days and my hair is matted in several places. I'd pass as an extra on the set of *The Walking Dead*.

Jesus, how much did I drink?

"Then just leave."

"I can do that?"

"You can do what you want. I don't give a guy my digits if he was a shitty lay. I'm out of there before he wakes up." I hear the deep voice of a guy in the background but can't make out what he's saying. "You do that thing with your tongue again and I'll give you my email address, too."

"I'm going to assume you were talking to whatever man is currently naked in bed with you and not me," I deadpan.

"He's not totally naked. We've been having fun with Nutella." She giggles.

"Can we get back to my problem, please?" I lean my ass against the counter so my back is to the mirror since I have zero interest in seeing how in shambles I am right now.

"Just bail. Grab your shit and get the hell outta Dodge."

"It's not rude to do that?" I chew on the end of my finger.

"Who cares? You're never going to see this guy again."

"You're right. Okay, I've got to run before he shows back up."

"Go get your stride of pride on and call me later."

I set about gathering my clothes from the apartment. Apparently, I must've had a wild time removing them last night because I find my shirt in the living room. Which is really nice, by the way, with a cream area rug set over the hardwood floors.

A fireplace with built-ins on either side lends a cozy feeling to the space and if I weren't so afraid of falling asleep and being here when he got back, I'd totally sink into the large brown sofa and make it my bitch.

But I digress. My pants are in Cole's bedroom and I find one of my shoes by the front door and the other one I remember spotting in the bathroom. Now I just need to find my purse so I can race from the scene of the crime.

Again, I try to remember *anything* from my time here last night and I come up blank. I search around frantically, feeling as if there's some giant clock ticking down my impending doom in the background.

Oh, wait. There is. When I get to the kitchen I realize he actually does have a giant clock on the one wall, whose second hand is adding to the drama going on inside my head.

There. My purse sits on the counter and relief floods through me. I hurry over to it and search its depths for my wallet, wanting to know whether I have any cash left for public transit. After the amount of money I'm sure I spent at the bar last night, I need to pinch pennies. If I have no cash on me, I'll be forced to use Uber.

I shift a bunch of stuff around and don't see it. Shit. Did I lose my wallet last night? A shot of adrenaline surges, not at all helping my already queasy stomach.

I knew I should have never bought that maroon wallet. Something bright or neon would be easier to find in this cavernous purse. Tahlia and Lennon are always making fun of how heavy my bag is. What can I say? I like to be prepared.

Frustrated at how long this is taking, I start moving things out of my purse and onto the kitchen counter. My hand sanitizer, lipstick, and notebook are the first to go. Then my bottle of water, tampons, and the vibrator Lennon gave me the other night. I roll my eyes to myself as I set it on the cool granite.

Does she really expect me to use that thing and report back to her? Next goes my face powder, small brush, and then finally my hand closes around my wallet.

"Yay!" I cheer to myself. I unzip it and see that it still has almost as much cash as when I left my grandparents' house last night.

Did I not pay my tab? I inwardly groan, but there's nothing to be done about it now. Because I am absolutely, definitely, never ever seeing Cole again. I pray that whatever tab I ran up last night doesn't come out of his paycheck.

Shaking my head to myself, I grab everything and quickly shove it back into my purse, more than ready to make my departure.

With swift strides I reach the door and don't bother looking back as I march out of there, trying to keep what little pride I have left intact.

Turns out Cole lives on the top floor of a converted Victorian.

Since I'm not exactly sure where I am, I do the walk of shame to the nearest street corner to read the street names and get my bearings. Luckily when I see the crossroads I know where I am and if I walk a couple of blocks up, I'll be able to take the bus to my grandparents' house without transferring.

I say a small thank you to the universe that it's autumn, since fall in San Francisco means the temperature isn't a thousand and one degrees. The walk to the bus stop nearly does me in and if it was crazy hot on top of that the coroner would be outlining my body on the side of the road.

My head is still pounding, but thankfully there's no one else sitting on the bench, and so I plop down with my purse on my lap. Hopefully, the bus will be here soon. I reach in to retrieve my wallet so I can count out my fare and of course it's somehow wedged its way to the bottom of my bag again.

With a big sigh, I start hunting.

I find my wallet easily this time, but what I don't come upon is the bright pink sex toy Lennon gave me the other night. Where the hell is that thing? She'll kill me if I lose it. I search for another minute and come up empty. Wait . . .

No.

No!

There's no one there to witness it, but heat seeps into my cheeks as mortification sets in.

Fuck. Me.

I put the vibrator back in my purse after I found my wallet at Cole's house, right?

I frantically shuffle all the items around inside my purse then lay them out beside each other on the bus bench until my purse is empty. Still no vibrator.

A middle-aged man arrives at that moment, eyes me skeptically, and chooses to wait for the bus a few feet away rather than approach me. Can't say I blame him.

I sink to my knees in front of the bench. "This is not happening. This is not happening. This is not happening!" I push my hands through my hair as I rock back and forth, having my mini-breakdown.

I may or may not have had a one-night stand with a guy who could be a model, I have no idea what transpired but I know it likely wasn't my finest moment, and now I've left a sex toy on his kitchen counter.

Someone toss me a shovel so I can dig a hole and never come out.

"Are you okay, miss?" the man waiting for the bus says, though I notice he doesn't dare to take a step closer to me.

I start shoving everything back into my purse once again. "Sure. I'll be fine. Apparently, you can't *actually* die from embarrassment."

He nods, but says nothing and turns his attention back to the street. I'm sure he's willing the bus to come so he can get away from the crazy lady on the bench.

Sulking, I sit back down with my purse in my lap.

Yep. As much as I'd like a second round that I can remember with Cole, I will never, ever, under any circumstances be seeing him again.

*chapter*

# FIVE

A FTER I UNLOCK THE door to my grandparents' place, I twist the handle and open it as slowly and quietly as possible, hoping I can slip in unnoticed and pretend that I've been here all night. Instead of silence, I'm met with three short yips of a dog.

*What the hell?*

I pause for a second, wondering if I'm hearing things because my grandparents didn't own a dog the entire time I was growing up and they don't own one now.

But there it is again. Barking that tells me there's definitely a dog somewhere in the house. I push the door all the way open and as soon as my foot hits the hardwood flooring of the entryway, I'm assaulted by one foot of fur ball.

One look at this dog and I can tell he's trouble. He's barking excitedly and bouncing up and down as if I have a raw steak shoved in my pocket. He stops his incessant barking for a second and his tongue hangs out to the side, his short tail flapping back and forth.

My grandma, Edna, appears from the back of the house,

smiling like there isn't some deranged animal in our midst and I'm not coming in looking like I've been turning tricks down on Polk Street all night. "I see you've met Sparky." I look up at her in confusion. "Your grandpa and I agreed to house the dogs that the local shelter has no room for. Just until they can find owners for them. Sparky arrived here this morning."

She bends down to pet the mutt, but he turns toward her and growls before she can get close enough to put her hands on him. My grandma just smiles. Then Sparky turns his head at an angle and looks at me again like he's expecting me to do something.

I simply stare at the five pounds of fur at my feet.

"I think he likes you." I can hear the smile in my grandma's voice.

Ignoring her comment, I say, "How come I didn't know you were helping the shelter out?"

"I never mentioned it?"

"Um . . . no." I look over at her and she smiles again and shrugs.

"A friend of a friend introduced me to the shelter's owner and one thing led to another. Before I knew it, we had a rotating door of dogs coming in and out of the house." She laughs as if it's the most amusing thing in the world.

I glance down at the little powder puff. "How long is he here for?"

"That all depends on how long it takes someone to adopt him. Penny, the lady who runs the shelter, she said he doesn't take to many people. Though it seems he's rather fascinated with you." She chuckles and a small smile creeps onto my face.

Figures that the only male interested in me would be of the four-legged variety. Considering what happened with my last fling, that's probably a good thing.

I ignore Sparky's pleading expression—I swear the corners

of his eyes and mouth are tugging down now—and I look back over at my grandma.

"How's job-hunting going?"

I feel the weight of anxiety settle in over me and I do my best to push it away. "Not well. I applied to a bunch of places, but none of the jobs were really in my field."

She reaches out and pats my cheek the way she has since I was a little girl. "Not to worry. You're a smart girl. I know you'll find something."

I place my hand over hers and smile. "Thanks, Grandma. And thanks again for letting me stay here until I'm on my feet."

"You're welcome to stay as long as you need to." A soft smile spreads across her face.

I lean in and kiss her cheek. I'm so lucky to have her.

"I was just about to make some breakfast. Your grandpa is out on the balcony. Why don't you join him and you can eat with us?"

As much as I enjoy spending time with my grandparents, I need some recovery time. After spending the day before applying to menial jobs I'm way overqualified for, unpacking all my worldly belongings at my grandparents' house, and maybe or maybe not fooling around with a stranger, I feel like I'm on a bus with a one-way ticket to Loserville.

All I really feel like doing is wallowing in misery in my bed. Alone.

"Thanks, Grandma, but I think I'm just going to go lie down."

"I remember what it was like to be your age." She chuckles. "You go nurse that hangover."

I grimace and she turns and shuffles her way to the kitchen, still laughing to herself over some memory our conversation has reminded her of. I hadn't realized it when I first arrived, but her gait is much more that of an elderly person's than I remember from the last time I visited.

I store that knowledge in my memory bank to pull out and examine at a later date and head upstairs.

I quickly change into my LuLaRoe leggings and an over-sized t-shirt and then dig my phone out of my purse to see that I've missed some texts in the group chat I have going on with Lennon and Tahlia.

> Lennon: *You would not believe the cock on that guy from last night. I'm telling you Tinder is a fucking goldmine of monster cock.*
>
> Tahlia: *You need some serious help.*
>
> Lennon: *Puh-lease. Tell that to me when you've been banging Chase for twenty years.*
>
> Tahlia: *Hey!*
>
> Lennon: *You know I'm kidding. You'll live HEA and ride off into the sunset. I just prefer to ride. Period.*
>
> Tahlia: *Don't we all know it.*
>
> Lennon: *So Tahl, ask Whit what she did last night. LMAO*
>
> Tahlia: *OMG what's going on?*
>
> Tahlia: *Hello!? Someone tell me!*
>
> Tahlia: *Whit what gives?*

I chuckle and shake my head at their back and forth. My friends are an endless source of entertainment. Plopping back onto my bed, I stretch out to type my reply.

> Me: *Hey, just seeing this. I'm with Tahl though. You need help. :P*
>
> Lennon: *Whatevs. Tell Tahl where you called me from this morning.*

*Tahlia: Yes! Tell me!!!*

*Me: I went home with some guy but I can't exactly remember what happened because I was too drunk.*

*Tahlia: OMFG!*

*Lennon: First you mess around with your boss. Then you're having one-night stands. My little girl is growing up. \*sniff\* I knew you weren't as innocent as you seem.*

In my current mood, I don't need to be reminded of the indiscretion that ultimately led to losing my job. But knowing Lennon, I know she doesn't mean it as an insult.

*Tahlia: Low blow, girl.*

*Lennon: Are you kidding me? I respect the shit outta that! Take it when and where you want it.*

*Me: Yeah, just sucks when he decides to fire you instead of bang you. LOL*

*Tahlia: His loss.*

*Lennon: Damn straight.*

*Tahlia: You have to fill me in on all the details the next time I see you!*

*Me: For sure. Listen girls I really need to go rest now.*

*Tahlia: K, chat later.*

*Lennon: Later, ho.*

I let my phone fall from my fingers onto the mattress. I don't really want to relive another way I've let myself down, so

I'll be avoiding that conversation with Tahl for as long as possible.

The fresh start I was hoping for is beginning to lose some of its lustre.

*chapter*

# SIX

"*I* CANNOT BELIEVE YOU lost my vibrator!" Lennon whisper-shouts as we enter the restaurant, Bliss, one of the Webber family's many holdings.

"I'm sorry. It was a complete accident." I smooth down the front of my dress and take in the upscale room full of upscale people. Tahlia says they've closed the place for the night so that Chase's parents can host the engagement party.

"How do you lose a vibrator by accident?" she asks as we pass the coat check girl our jackets.

"It's a long story. I'll have to tell you later."

I finally came clean with her. Well, partly. I haven't exactly told her *how* I lost it. A few weeks have passed since she gave it to me and she's been harassing me wanting to know what I thought of its 'performance'. I figured the best place to tell her was when she couldn't ask me too many follow-up questions. Surely even Lennon wouldn't go Bruce Lee on my ass and embarrass Tahlia in front of all of San Francisco's elite.

I'll be honest. Most of the people here are not my kind of people. We're not a part of the same tribe. At all. They're all

dressed in designer duds that cost more than a month's rent—
which in San Francisco is a shit ton—and my dress came off the
rack at Target. While they assume the world will bend to their
will, I'm more than aware that life isn't fair.

Tahlia's parents have never been anything other than outwardly cordial to me, but I know if they could choose, they'd
have had her be besties with one of the daughters of their coun-
try-club buddies.

That's not to say that I don't like Chase. I like him enough,
I suppose. Though it was a different story when he and Tahlia
first got together, he's grown on me and my friend is happy, so
who am I to say who she should marry?

The Webber family is well regarded in the Bay area, though
I never really could understand why. They're constantly buying
up and shutting down low-rent buildings to build high-end real
estate. To me, they prey upon the little guys in order to stuff
their pockets and I have zero respect for that. Still, I can grin and
bear it for an evening if it means it'll make Tahl happy.

"I can't wait to hear this story," Lennon says. We step away
from the coat check and look around for our girl. "Did you lose
it up your hooha?"

I turn to face her. "My what?"

"Your hooha. You know, your va-jay-jay? Your C-U-next-
Tuesday . . ."

I roll my eyes and smile as I see Tahlia and Chase approaching.

"There's my girls!" Tahl says, embracing us each in a quick
hug before pulling back to take us in. She looks gorgeous in a
champagne-colored dress that hits just above her knee. She's
left her blond locks down with large curls in them. "You both
look beautiful. Don't they look beautiful, Chase?" She turns to
look at her fiancé.

Chase stands behind Tahl and places his hands on both her

shoulders, squeezing. "You ladies look lovely as always."

"Congratulations, Chase. I haven't seen you since I heard the big news."

"Yeah, congrats," Lennon adds.

"Thank you. I'm a lucky man." Tahlia turns her head to the side, and they lock gazes for a moment. It's apparent how much they care for one another. I ignore the little stab of envy in my chest.

"Where's your mom?" Lennon asks. "You know I love torturing her. I plan to sidle up to her and strike up a conversation as soon as the mayor makes his way over to her."

Tahlia chuckles while Chase stifles a grin. "Last I saw her she was speaking to the priest over there." She gestures in the general direction of the bar and Lennon takes off, her head thrown back while she fakes some type of maniacal laughter.

Tahlia just rolls her eyes and returns her attention to me. "How's job-hunting going? Any luck so far?"

I shrug. "I had an interview earlier this week. Don't think it's going to go anywhere. But I have a lead on a job at WHFI News that I'm excited about." I know she's being a good friend by asking, but this is the last thing I want to talk about right now. I want to keep my mood light and celebratory in honor of my friend.

"That's so wonderful!" Tahlia exclaims.

Chase gives a nod of approval. I suppose working for the local news is deemed acceptable in his social circle. Why did I think that? That's mean.

"I doubt anything will come of it . . ."

"Nonsense." Tahlia reaches forward and swats my upper arm. "They'd be lucky to have you."

"We'll see."

"Would you two excuse me for a second? I just spotted my brother and I need to go over something with him," Chase says and gives Tahlia a peck on the cheek.

I stiffen a bit at the mention of Chase's brother.

Her exuberant expression falls a smidgen. "Work? At our engagement party? Really, Chase?"

"Well, if he'd ever get back to me with the details he's supposed to during business hours, I wouldn't have to corner him at social functions. I'll send him over when we're done talking so he can apologize to you."

Tahlia sighs and Chase walks away without saying anything more.

"You okay?" I asked.

"It's just Chase's brother. He can be so . . . what am I saying? You know what he's like because—"

I raise my hand before she goes any further. "That's something I'm not keen on reliving."

"Fair enough." Her lips press together. "You'll be okay being around him after what happened?"

"It was years ago, Tahl. I'm over it," I lie. Chase's brother made his way to the top of my shit list years ago, when he stood me up on a blind date, and he hasn't budged from that spot since, but she doesn't need to know that. I can grin and bear it for the sake of my friend.

"He's still a perpetual bachelor, you know. Man whore. Unapologetic. Doesn't follow through on anything. You dodged a bullet, believe me. Chase says him and his dad have really been butting heads lately."

"Sounds like you're marrying the right brother then."

Tahlia gives a small laugh. "That's for damn sure." Smoothing her hands over her hair, she puts her party face back on.

"You go mingle. I'm going to get a drink from the bar and rescue your mom from Lennon."

"Thank you!" Tahlia leans forward to embrace me. "You're the best."

I don't feel like I'm the best because the idea of meeting Tahlia's soon-to-be brother-in-law makes me want to slip out of here unnoticed. What he did to me that night so many years ago was bad enough. He hadn't even met me before, but he was so cruel by leaving me sitting alone at a restaurant waiting for my date to show up. I had an instant distaste for him, but I could have gotten over it. It was everything that happened after I stepped out of the restaurant that night. The trajectory of my life changed in an instant and I fully blamed him.

Biting back my unease, I smile and turn to push my way through the crowd. I recognize a few of Tahlia's cousins in the room and some of the more well-known people in San Francisco, though if I hadn't been gone for a few years I'd likely recognize more.

There. I see Lennon across the room talking to Mrs. Santora, who looks like she can't get away from her fast enough. With a grin to myself I step up to the bartender, an attractive woman in her mid-twenties with long, wavy brown hair. The tips of her hair are dyed much lighter and though my hair is darker than hers and shoulder-length, I wonder if that's something I can pull off.

"What can I get you this evening?" she asks.

Before I can answer a deep, familiar voice that sends shivers up my spine and heat to my nether regions speaks from behind me.

"If memory serves, the lady enjoys her whiskey."

Every muscle in my body seizes. I let my eyes drift shut, hoping and praying the voice doesn't belong to who I think it does.

Slowly, as if I'm a car in the middle of a showroom floor, I pivot around to face the person behind me.

Cole.

Complete and total mortification consumes every cell in my body, painting my skin red, and I wish for another 1906 earthquake to happen so I can be swallowed up whole.

"What the hell are you doing here?"

Granted, it's not the best thing to say to him, but it's the first thing that comes out of my mouth. And let's be honest. It's what I'm really thinking.

His forehead crinkles in on itself and a crease forms between his eyes as he studies me for a second. He opens his mouth to respond, but right that second Chase steps up.

"Whitney, I see you've met my brother." He clamps Cole on the shoulder and looks at me with a smile.

I stand there like an idiot, gaping at the two of them, my gaze darting between them. The family resemblance is clear now that I see them side by side.

"Cole, we need to talk," a deep baritone snips from beside our group.

We all glance over to who I recognize from the newspapers is Cole and Chase's father, Winston Webber.

"I'm in the middle of a conversation, it'll have to wait." Cole's intense stare is back on me again. I glance at him quickly and can't manage to hold his stare so I return my attention to his father.

"Yes, I know you always have time to chat up a pretty girl, but business doesn't always wait. It's your brother's engagement party, for Christ's sakes, and you don't see him complaining."

I feel bad for the way that Cole's father is speaking to him in front of everyone and that on top of everything else makes me bolt.

"Excuse me."

Without further thought or a backward glance I bolt from our small group, desperate to disappear.

I stumble into an expansive bathroom with long granite counters and floor-to-ceiling wood doors that make up the bathroom stalls. All of which are open. Seems like the big guy upstairs has cut me a break because now that I'm alone I can really lose my shit.

*Tahlia is going to kill me.*

I've listened to her talk about what a man whore Chase's brother is, how entitled he is, how he's nothing more than a pampered rich guy who thinks the world should fall at his feet. But I already knew all that because of what happened between us. Or what didn't, to be more accurate.

I slink down into one of the comfortable-looking chairs in the lounge area of the bathroom. I can't fathom why I even gave someone like him the time of day.

Before this moment, I'd always wondered why the hell they put these mini-living rooms in the hoity-toity bathrooms. I mean, who wants to hang out near a public toilet? I guess it's for moments like these, when you find out you may or may not have slept with your best friend's soon-to-be brother-in-law who you grew to hate years before because of what he did to you.

Oh, and let's not forget the whole vibrator thing.

I groan and cover my eyes as that realization comes to mind.

I hear the creak of the door hinges and hurriedly lower my hands, sitting up straight trying to look . . . oh, I don't know . . . like I'm composed and just choosing to hang out in the bathroom by myself instead of at the party.

Heels click on the marble floor as they make their way down the short hallway into the restroom.

"Lennon!" I've never been more relieved to see her. I need someone to talk me off the ledge and tell me it's all going to be okay.

She turns her head and notices me as she's striding by and does a quick spin on her four-inch heels, joining me in the makeshift living room.

"What the hell are you doing?" She glances around the bathroom to make sure we're alone. "Did you just get it on with someone in here?" Her eyes light with mischief and she waggles her eyebrows.

I shake my head at her. "You really need help."

"What's going on then?" Concern dots her expression now and she takes a seat in the plush chair beside me.

I swallow past the large lump forming in my throat. Is this what a cat feels like when they're working out a hairball?

I remind myself that I can't bother being distracted until I figure out a way to face Cole again with my pride intact. What can I say? Wishful thinking on my part.

"I just met Chase's brother, Cole."

A smile broadens on her face. "Oh, yeah. I met him earlier. Day-um. The things I could do to that man with twenty-four hours, some rope, and lube." She looks off into the distance as if she's picturing it in her mind.

I ignore the pang of jealousy worming its way into my chest at the idea of Lennon and Cole together. "I think I may have already . . . hit it."

Lennon's mouth drops open, but she says nothing.

Note the date and time on the calendar, folks. The fact that I've left Lennon speechless is worth keeping record of.

"The bartender I went home with . . . it was Cole." Lennon's still staring at me with wide eyes and not speaking so I continue. "I thought he was the freaking bartender, for Christ's sakes!"

She gives her head a shake as if she's coming out of a trance. "Holy shit, Whit!" Gripping both my shoulders, she gives them a little shake then lets her hands drop. "Hey, that rhymes," she says as almost an afterthought.

"I can't believe I didn't put two and two together." I'm now wringing my hands in my lap.

A small frown forms on her face. "Oh, please. It doesn't sound like you asked for his last name, how could you know? There's probably hundreds or even thousands of Coles in the city."

"I guess, but . . ." I let a frustrated growl escape. "Why did it have to be him, of all people? This whole situation is such a mess," I say and slump back into the chair.

Lennon breaks out in laughter. "You did a fuck-and-chuck to him. I love it." She raises her hand as if to give me a high five. "Girl power!"

I simply stare at her hand as another crushing blow to my fragile ego hits. "I'm a Webber wench! Oh, my God!"

My friend presses her lips together like she's trying not to laugh.

Ever since Tahlia began dating Chase and we heard about some of the antics his older brother would get up to we'd always laughed and joked about the many women he'd bang and call them 'Webber wenches'. I'd felt only pity for those girls as we'd all laugh at how stupid they were to think they'd be anything special to a man who traded them like baseball cards. If I'm honest, I'd always felt a little superior to that type of girl. And now I've joined their ranks.

Karma really is a fucking bitch.

"Apparently, there's low, ten miles of shit, rock bottom, and then sludge below that. I'm swimming in the sludge right now, Lennon."

She adjusts herself closer to the end of her chair and leans forward to embrace me. "No, you're not. You're just having a rough time, that's all. It will get better."

I let my head rest on her tatted shoulder and pray she's right. "I hope so." After a few seconds, I continue. "We can't let Tahlia know about this." We pull apart and looked at each other. "I hate keeping secrets from anyone, but this is supposed to be one of the happiest times of her life. This will only stress her out."

I see it in Lennon's eyes, the moment she remembers what he did to me. "He's the one who . . ."

"Exactly. Tahlia will be even more worried about whether

I'm okay being around Cole during all her wedding stuff. I don't want to burden her. Whatever did or did not happen between us won't happen again, so it's a moot point. Cole Webber is not the type of man I want in my life or my bed."

"I don't know what's wrong with you. He's exactly the type of man I'd want in my bed."

I smacked Lennon playfully on the arm. "Would you be serious for a minute?"

She holds both her hands up in front of her to placate me. "Okay, okay. Seriously, though, I agree with you. Tahl is better off not knowing. Her mother is going to drive her batshit crazy during this entire wedding planning process wanting to make sure everything is perfect and up to her standards. She doesn't need the extra stress."

I nod and draw in a big breath. "So, how should I play this with him? What do I say? Do I bring up what happened before?"

Lennon chews her bottom lip for a second, deep in thought. "Act like it's no big deal. Explain that you didn't know who he was, but now that you do you'd appreciate it if he didn't tell anyone about it because it will make things awkward, and absolutely do not bring up the past. It will only make it worse."

I nod with more enthusiasm this time. "Right. I can do that."

"And then you have to *not* be awkward."

My shoulders slump. "That's going to be a lot harder."

She raises herself from the seat and adjusts her tight, bright blue dress. "Come on. You can do this."

I sure as hell hope she's right. I stand from the chair, straighten my shoulders, lift my chin and mentally prepare myself to go out there and have a conversation with Cole fucking Webber as if his presence here doesn't faze me one bit.

My heels click on the hard floor as Lennon follows me down the hall.

"Just keep reminding yourself you can't sleep with him

again while you're talking to him. The guy is like the opposite of Medusa. Instead of turning to stone you turn to mush."

"I only make my mistakes once." I turn to face her as I use my ass to push open the bathroom door behind me. "It will be a cold day in hell before I'd ever let a guy like Cole Webber get in my pants again. Obviously, it wasn't earth-shattering enough the first time around if I can't even remember it."

Now, had I known Cole was standing there waiting for me to leave the ladies' room, overhearing every word I said, I probably would have phrased it a little differently.

*chapter*

# SEVEN

I TAKE A STEP into the hallway as heat races up into my neck and face. I must be the color of an overripe tomato right now.

Cole's jaw is clenched and his forehead is creased. I'm able to *really* look at him now. He's clean-shaven this time around and dressed in an expensive-looking charcoal suit with an azure silk tie. He sure as hell cleans up well. In no way does he remind me of the laid-back, working man I met in the bar. Tonight, he oozes sophistication and fits right in with the rest of the country-clubbers circulating the room outside this hallway comparing their bank accounts.

He pushes off the wall he was leaning against and takes a couple of steps toward me, his body rigid and tense.

Lennon, that bitch, doesn't even stick around to be my wingwoman. Instead she slinks off down the hall back to the party.

"My apologies if the other night wasn't memorable for you. It makes things difficult when you're working with a lush."

So, this is how we're going to play this? Sure thing. I've got years of pent-up anger and resentment toward this man and he doesn't even know it.

Let's do this.

"Maybe I felt the need to be intoxicated in order to get through it."

He gives me such a condescending laugh that I now know beyond all doubt that I must have been *very* handsy that night. Damn whiskey. "Nice try, sweetheart." He leans in a little closer to me and I can smell his expensive cologne. "You were *begging* me for it."

I let my hands drop and clench them at my sides. "You lied."

His eyebrows arch up. "Excuse me?"

"You lied."

The crease in his forehead deepens. "How did I lie?"

"You let me believe that you were just a bartender."

"Who's to say I'm not just a bartender?" He clenches that stupid strong jaw of his.

"You're Cole fucking Webber."

He closes the few inches between us and the smell of his cologne hits me and I fight not to let my eyes flutter closed. He's so close that I have to crank my neck back to look at him. "What the hell is that supposed to mean?"

"Oh, please. Is this the part where you play the poor, misunderstood rich boy? I'm not buying it."

"You don't know shit about me," he practically growls.

"I know you have zero regard for anyone else's feelings. You're used to taking what you want when you want it. You toss people aside when you feel like it and to hell with them."

He squeezes his eyes shut for a second and uses his thumb and finger to rub the bridge of his nose. "Are you on some kind of medication or something? Because you're making zero fucking sense."

Of course, I'm not making any sense. He wouldn't remember me, but how could I forget *him*?

"Had I known who you really were I wouldn't have let you get within ten feet of me."

A small smirk plays at the corner of his mouth before he leans down and says right into my ear, "Now, now, Whit." He pronounces the 't' at the end of my name extra hard to exaggerate the fact that he's using my nickname. "We both know it wouldn't have mattered who I was that night. You were looking for some cock. I was happy to give it to you and you were more than happy to receive it."

I suck in a startled gasp. "You're exaggerating," I say in a breathy voice that does nothing to back up my argument.

He chuckles, the sensation of his breath on my neck and ear causing shivers to race down my arm. Thankfully, he moves back and gives me some room. Unthankfully, his hazel eyes bore into me like lasers and I'm unable to look away. "Not exaggerating, no." He shakes his head. "What was it you called mine when you grabbed it? Oh, yeah. Unicorn cock. I still don't understand the reference, but I do know it must mean I have one magical cock."

I'm going to go ahead and blame Lennon here for even putting unicorns in my head with that stupid van of hers. And Jesus, would he stop saying 'cock' already? It's an aphrodisiac when it comes from his mouth and I'm doing my best to remember that I am no longer allowed to be attracted to this man.

I clench my teeth for a full minute and just stare at him and the shit-eating grin plastered on his face.

Before I can think of a scathing response Chase comes sauntering down the hallway toward the restrooms. "You guys look like you're in the middle of an intense conversation," he says.

I turn my gaze away from Cole and look to Chase and smile.

"Whitney was just telling me how fond she is of unicorns," Cole says with a straight face.

My cheeks burn, but I don't take the bait.

"Have you seen Lennon's van lately?" Chase asks me. "You

should take a ride in that thing if you're a fan of unicorns." He laughs.

"Have you ridden a unicorn before, Whit?" Cole asks. If I weren't so irritated with the man right now I'd almost call his smile playful, but since I am irritated I'm going to go ahead and describe it as provoking.

With a saccharine smile, I respond. "I think I have. Hard to say really. It must not have been as memorable as you'd expect."

And with that comment I head off down the hall with an exaggerated sway to my hips, because if I still want Cole Webber after everything he did to me all those years ago, and everything I know about him, I'm going to make doubly sure he feels the same.

Misery does love company, after all.

## chapter

# EIGHT

*I* DIDN'T SPEND ANY more time *talking* to Cole at the engagement party, though I felt his gaze on me more than once. I did, however, spend a lot of time *thinking* about Cole after the party. Which is really frustrating since all I wanted to do was to get him out of my mind.

It's probably just because he's so damn infuriating.

You know how sometimes all your best comebacks come to you *after* you've had a fight with someone? I couldn't stop thinking of what I should have said and one-line zingers that would have really pissed him off.

Mature, I know.

Tahlia called earlier and invited me to dinner with her and Chase tonight. All day I've been worried that they caught wind of something between Cole and me. I'm not sure what to say if they confront me about it. Somehow, "Yes, we might have slept together, I'm not really sure, but I still want his body, I just hate the person he is" doesn't seem to cut it.

The moment of truth is upon me as I park my grandma's car (since she let me borrow it) and walk into the restaurant.

Of course, we're at one of the Webber-owned restaurants. After making a fortune in land deals around the city on the backs of the less fortunate, they've expanded their holdings to include several restaurants in the Bay area.

Sapphron has an easy, relaxed feel to it with tone-on-tone cream and beige decor, a wide-open main room that looks into the kitchen, and large comfortable-looking chairs at the tables. The sign outside says their specialty is California cuisine, as fitting as it is unoriginal.

My tummy is in knots as I try to come up with all the reasons I might have been summoned here tonight. Tahl wouldn't give me any info on the phone so I'm going in blind. She seemed a little cagey when I asked what was up, but she just said we'd discuss it at dinner.

"Can I help you, miss?" the maître d' asks.

"Yes, I'm meeting Chase Webber and his fiancée."

He nods. "Very well. The happy couple are already seated. Follow me, please."

I follow as he leads the way through the tables of happy diners and smile when Tahlia waves to me from a table near the back of the room. It's overlooking the city and you can see the lights from the Golden Gate Bridge in the distance, a view that never fails to take my breath away.

I'm not quite sure what happens next. One minute I'm glancing at the view outside and the next I'm sailing through the air and the floor is rapidly approaching my face. In an attempt to save myself from a broken nose I reach for the first thing I see, which happens to be the table next to me. Instead of grabbing onto a solid surface though, I clutch a thin piece of material and it follows me down to the ground.

Somehow, I manage to get my hands out in front of me to brace myself and I land with a thud on the ground, followed by what feels like every dish that was on the table landing on my back, covering me with what I can only guess is someone's dinner and drinks.

The room lets out a collective gasp at my misfortune.

"Whit!" Tahlia shrieks and I hear her push her chair back.

"Miss, are you okay?" I look up into the horrified eyes of the maître d', who seems unsure as to whether he should help me out by removing the plates off my back.

"Oh, my God!" Tahlia stands behind him and looks ready to push past to help when a low voice from behind me has me wanting to sink into the earth below.

"Jonah, please grab the bus boy to clean up this mess and grab these nice people whatever they were having on the house. I'll help Miss Knight up."

You have got to be kidding me. What is Cole doing here? He's like a bad fucking zit, always popping up when you least want him to.

Cole removes the few remaining dishes from my back. "Here," he says as he helps me to my feet. I can feel some type of warm liquid dripping off the back of my skirt and onto my leg.

"Jeez, Whit. Are you all right?" Tahlia asks.

"I'm fine. The only thing hurt is my pride." I spin to look at Cole for the first time and it's all I can do to keep my breath in my body.

He's wearing a black dress shirt with the top couple of buttons undone. The sleeves are rolled up to reveal his muscled forearms. Dark slacks hug his hips and his hair is a little messy, but somehow manages to look like he meant for it to be that way.

After clearing my throat, I manage to get out my question. "Is there somewhere I can clean up?"

"Of course. Follow me."

"I can take her," Tahlia offers.

Cole shakes his head. "I've got it covered. Why don't you and Chase order us some appetizers?"

She nods, though a little apprehensively. "Yeah, okay."

My gaze flicks back to Chase who's watching us, but is still seated at the table. Really? He couldn't even be bothered to get up?

And wait . . . I'm just realizing that the way Cole said that made it sound as if he'd be joining us.

"Follow me."

I do as Cole says and make my way through the dining area, careful not to make eye contact with any of the patrons. I don't need to see them to know that they're either looking at me with pity or distaste.

Cole leads me through a swinging door and into a bustling kitchen. I get a few strange looks from the employees, but no one says anything as we make our way down a hall and into a small office.

"Stay here," Cole orders and turns and leaves me there.

I make a face behind his back after he's gone. Who is he to boss me around?

I look around the office and recognize Cole's scrawl on some of the papers on the corner of the desk. The room isn't large and it's overflowing with paper and restaurant supplies. A chair sits behind the desk, but it's the only one in the small office.

After a few minutes, he returns with a bowl of water and a white towel, a white dress shirt slung over his shoulder.

"Take your shirt off," he says as he sets the bowl down on the desk.

As much as his command sends a thrill through me, I'm not about to admit it to him. I cock a hip and cross my arms over my chest. "Excuse me?" I tried to use my most offended voice, but I'm afraid it may have come out a little too breathy to pull it off.

"You heard me. Take it off and I'll wipe your back down."

"You think I'm just going to take off my shirt in front of you?"

"It's nothing I haven't seen before, Whit." He arches a brow and turns to close the office door behind him. It doesn't escape my notice that he locked it, too.

Embarrassment turns my face hot. "Whitney. You haven't earned the privilege of calling me Whit."

"Whatever, Whitney." He exaggerates saying my name. "Let's go. I want to get this dinner over with. I have things to do after."

"I think you mean people, not things," I grumble as I turn my back to him. Inhaling a deep breath, I reach for my hem and pull the light sweater I'm wearing up over my head. The fabric is still wet and I try my best not to transfer any of whatever it is into my hair. "There."

I can't see it, but I'm sure Cole is rolling his eyes at me behind my back.

"Is it on my skirt at all?"

"A little, but I should be able to wipe most of it off. Since it's black you'll hardly notice after."

I hear the water in the bowl trickle as he wrings out the cloth and without any further warning his hands are on me. Well, the cloth is, but that's only leaving his hands millimeters from my skin so that's almost the same thing.

My spine stiffens and my heart races while I stand there as straight and stiff as a two-by-four. He wipes my back and rinses the cloth again. When he uses one hand to lift my bra strap and wipe underneath it I suck in a breath. A cloudy memory comes to mind of the two of us kissing and his hand slipping under the elastic of my bra strap.

I shake my head in an attempt to push the memory from my mind. I'd prefer to continue to remember nothing from that night.

When Cole is done he pats my back dry with a towel in such a gentle way you'd think he had a sensitive bone in his body.

He doesn't fool me for a second.

"I always keep a clean dress shirt here in case I need to be in the front of the house when I come to check in on things. You can put this on if you want."

He's still standing behind me and I'm able to feel his body heat seeping into me, making me warm inside. Cole's fingertips lightly run across my shoulder and tingles follow in their wake, electrifying me and my libido.

"Thanks," I say in a soft voice. I turn slightly and reach for the shirt and shrug it on. I don't turn back around to face him until I've done up most of the buttons. The shirt is way too big for me, so I tie the bottom in a knot, hoping it will look purposeful and maybe even a little fashionable. "I didn't realize you were joining us for dinner." I try to keep the animosity from my voice because he did just help me out, but I'm not sure I succeeded entirely.

"Chase said he wanted to go over some wedding stuff with me." He shrugs. "I wasn't expecting you either."

I scoff and try to roll up one of the sleeves, but it's hard with just one hand.

"Here, let me."

Begrudgingly I hold my arm out and Cole slowly folds up the sleeves, his gaze darting between what he's doing with his hands and my face. I somehow manage to keep an impassive expression.

I'm surrounded by his scent and catch myself inhaling deeper to bask in it. His gaze darts to my lips a few times and I resist the urge to lean in and kiss him. Because damn it. Why would I want this man to kiss me after everything that happened in my life because of him?

He finishes up and takes a step back from me, his hands on his hips. "You do naughty secretary well."

I roll my eyes and grab my purse off the desk. "Can we

go now?"

His face hardens instantly. "What is your problem? Seriously?"

"My only problem right now is that I want out of here and you're standing in front of the door."

He shakes his head. "That doesn't explain why your mood soured so much when you found out I was Chase's brother. And don't tell me it has anything to do with me not being just a bartender. Most girls would be happy to find out I wasn't just a working Joe."

"Well, I'm not that girl, I suppose." I move to take a step forward and he raises a hand to stop me.

"Suit yourself. But if you're not going to tell me, at least drop the bitch act. It doesn't suit you." He spins on his heel and swings the door open forcibly.

I raise my chin and follow behind him, trying to stitch together the small part of my dignity that's left as I walk with fake confidence back through the dining room. I need this night to be over. Sitting across from Cole all evening pretending he doesn't affect me is going to take its toll. I just want it over and done with.

"Are you okay?" Tahlia looks so concerned as I take the seat across from her. Cole holds the chair out for me and pushes it in after I've sat down.

"Thank you," I mutter then direct my attention back to Tahl. "I'm fine. Apparently utter mortification can't actually kill you." I give her a small smile.

She reaches across the table to squeeze my hand. "I can't believe that happened." She looks like she wants to laugh so I let her off the hook and smile a genuine smile at her. Sure enough a small giggle escapes.

Chase interrupts us a moment later. "All right, let's start dinner. I have to swing back by the office."

Tahlia shoots him a look and straightens in her chair then motions the waiter over to us.

*⟳~ℓℓᵖ*

LATER ON, THE WAITER has just cleared the table of our appetizers when an awkward silence descends.

Cole leans back in his chair and it's hard not to notice how that action stretches the fabric over his muscled chest. He catches me admiring him and I immediately glance away, not interested in seeing the satisfied grin I'm sure is spreading across his face.

"So, why exactly have you two summoned us here tonight? I have to assume it has something to do with the wedding?" Cole asks.

"We didn't *summon* you," Chase says with no small amount of irritation in his voice.

Cole scoffs. "You asked me to join you, I told you I had somewhere I needed to be, and you insisted that I be here anyway. What would you call it?" Cole stares at his younger brother, his mouth in a straight line.

"Well, we want to thank you both for being here," Tahlia says, ever the good hostess and peacemaker.

"Of course," I say, meaning it. Even though being around Cole is the last thing I want, Tahlia is one of my best friends and I'd do anything for her.

"We've set a date for the wedding," Chase says.

"That's amazing!" I glance over at my friend and she's beaming. "When is it?"

"Well . . . that's the thing." She's playing with her wine glass on the table, spinning the base around and around, and it makes me think she's nervous. "You know how I've always wanted to have my reception at the Julia Morgan Ballroom, right?"

I nod my head. Tahlia, or maybe her mother more

accurately, has been planning her wedding since she was a young girl and she's never wavered in her desire to have her reception at San Francisco's most exclusive special events venue.

"Well, we inquired about a date and it turns out they're completely booked up on spring and summer weekends for the next few years. But . . . they did have a couple recently cancel. The only problem is that it's about nine months away. May to be exact."

"That's quick," Cole says.

"That's where you guys come in," Chase responds.

"We don't want to have to wait three years to get married and so, as maid of honor and best man, we're hoping we can count on you guys for help."

Wait, Cole is the best man? This is the first I've heard of this little nugget of information.

"What do you need?" I ask.

"We're hoping that we can pass along some of the smaller jobs to you two. We're both so busy at work, it's going to be hard to run around the city and get everything done in time."

I ignore the pang in my chest over her work comment because I know she doesn't mean I have all the time in the world because I don't have a job. I'm just being ultra-sensitive.

"I thought your mom would've hired the best wedding planner in the city." I pick up my glass of wine and take a small sip.

"She tried, but this lady doesn't know her ass from a hole in the ground. I'm not comfortable leaving everything in her hands."

Tahlia confessed once that what she really wanted to be if she hadn't felt pressured to join the family business was an event planner, so I'm guessing Tahl is a tough customer to please.

"Can we count on you?" I think Chase is directing that question to both of us, but he's looking at his brother with a pointed stare.

"Of course you can. Whit and I are more than happy to

help out the happy couple. Aren't we?" Cole's hand clamps down on my shoulder and I inhale a quick breath as the warmth seeps into my skin. What Tahl and Chase can't see, but I can feel, is the way Cole is rubbing his thumb back and forth over my skin.

I glance over at him and he's wearing a shit-eating grin and I know it's because he's aware of how his touch is affecting me.

Since I can't get into it with him in front of Tahl and Chase, I merely give him a small smile and say, "Of course."

"Great." Tahlia claps her hands together in front of her. "I knew we could count on you guys."

"We'll do whatever it takes."

As the words leave my mouth I know I mean them, but at the same time I can't help the feeling that I both dread and look forward to exactly what that will entail.

*chapter*

# NINE

I PLOP FACE FIRST onto my bed as soon as I get home, letting out a groan that probably makes it sound as if I'm in pain.

I'm not. Not really. Truth is I'm trying to figure out how I'm going to spend so much time around Cole without ripping either his head or his clothes off. The guy is an arrogant ass and I refuse to be his plaything for however long I interest him, only to be tossed aside when he's had his fill.

A scratching on the other side of the door has me pushing up off the mattress and walking to the other side of the room to see what the hell that sound is.

Sparky.

I forgot about that little guy.

He comes right on in as if he's been invited. Which, he most certainly has not.

"What do you want, powder puff?"

He sits down at my feet, little tail wagging and his small pink tongue hanging out of one side of his mouth.

"What?" I have next to no experience with dogs since my

grandparents didn't have any growing up. I have no idea what this mutt wants.

*Arf.*

"Shhh, you're going to wake everyone up."

*Arf.*

"Shh," I say again and bend over to pet him in case that's what he's looking for. Sparky closes his eyes like he's in bliss. As soon as I pull away his eyes snap back open and I swear if pets have expressions his is saying, *What they hell are you stopping for?*

I ignore his silent plea and lie back on the bed, drawing in a deep breath before weighing my options.

After I left the restaurant Tahl called me to ask if I was *really* okay working with Cole and I assured her I was.

I could fess up and tell her what happened with Cole and explain why, on top of what happened years ago, I'm uncomfortable having to spend a lot of time with him. Tahlia will understand, but it will cause her more stress in what I'm sure will be an already stressful time in her life. Especially since the wedding is now so close.

Or I can be an adult about it and put my feelings for Cole aside—both the irritation and the attraction that I seem to feel when it comes to San Francisco's foremost bachelor. I close my eyes and try to picture myself being around Cole. Having to text Cole. Run things by Cole. It will be difficult, but not impossible. Surely, I can toe the line and not allow the two of us to either fall in bed with each other (because I don't really think Tahlia would be happy about that), or become mortal enemies (because I *know* Tahlia wouldn't be happy about that).

I hear some high-pitched whimpering from the floor so I roll onto my side and see Sparky still there. At his feet is the blouse I had on earlier that had all the food spilled on it. Anger heats my face. It's shredded into a bunch of different pieces. There's no saving it. Death by dog.

Sparky must have pulled it out of my tote purse on the floor and chowed down.

"Bad dog," I scold.

He hangs his head in what I guess must be shame and I feel a little guilty. But really, he's just ruined one of my nicer pieces. One I can't afford to replace.

I roll onto my back again and let out a big puff of air. So far things haven't been exactly what I expected when I moved home to San Francisco. I figured I'd find a job right away, spend my nights out with the girls, live life like I was back in college. Instead Tahlia's getting married, Lennon's off getting laid and trying to build a sex toy empire, and I have a small rodent destroying my clothing.

Something catches my eye and I turn to see Sparky jumping up and down beside the bed.

Huh. I didn't even know dogs could jump straight up like that.

He eyeballs me every time he comes eye level with the bed, but he's not able to jump high enough to make it onto the mattress.

"Do you want on the bed?"

*Arf.*

I'm going to assume that's a yes and so the next time he's airborne I reach out with both hands and catch the little squirmer mid-flight then set him gently on the bed.

"Is this what you wanted?"

In answer, he leans in and licks my face.

"Gross." I wipe the dog saliva off my cheek with the sleeve of Cole's shirt. I probably should have changed out of it as soon as I arrived home. Should have. But didn't.

Sparky licks me again as soon as I've removed all traces of him from my cheek.

"Stop that," I say with a laugh. The mangy mutt must think

I like it because he tries to lick me again. This time I'm quicker and I pick him up and place him back on the floor.

*Arf.*

"Shh."

*Arf.*

I sigh. "Fine, you can come back up, but you can't lick me, you understand? If you do you're going back on the floor, got it?"

Sparky sits and wags his tail furiously.

I reach down and lift him back up on the mattress. This time instead of heading for my face he curls in beside me and lies down. I let him stay there because he looks comfortable and it doesn't seem worth it to bother him. That's what I tell myself anyway, because it absolutely cannot be that I find this little mongrel somewhat cute.

I know what I have to do.

I have to suck it up and find some way to work with Cole. Before that can happen, we need to come to an understanding. An agreement of sorts.

We're both adults, so it shouldn't be that hard, right?

*chapter*

# TEN

*M*AKE-UP. CHECK.

Cute hair. Check.

Skinny jeans. Check.

Fitted shirt that shows my curves. Check.

My final once-over in the mirror doesn't exactly reveal me to be femme fatale status, but if I do say so myself, I look attractive and at least I'm not stinking drunk or covered in a plateful of food. Progress.

A soft knock at the door has me turning in that direction. My grandma pokes her head through with a knowing smile. "Honey, there's a nice boy at the door to see you." I crook my head and scrunch my forehead. "Pretty sure he said his name is Cole."

*What the hell is he doing here?*

After coming to terms with the fact that I would have to make nice with Cole, I got his number from Tahlia under the guise that I would need it to help with the wedding. I texted and asked if he wanted to meet. We're *supposed* to be meeting at Golden Gate Park in half an hour. I figured a neutral meeting spot sans alcohol would be best.

"He's here? At the front door?"

She simply nods and turns, leaving my room.

I scramble to grab my purse, slip on my shoes, and in seconds I'm bounding down the stairs.

Cole is at the front door speaking with my grandpa and he turns his head and smiles at me when he hears me. And what a smile it is.

I swear I hear angels singing and the clouds part, casting sunlight all over him through the glass of the front door. This man is too much. Too much everything—confidence, beauty, swagger, and anything else that describes a person who makes your breath hitch every time you see him.

"What are you doing here?" I ask him and his smile falters. Just a bit at the corner, but I don't miss it.

My grandma reaches out and lightly smacks my arm. "Whitney, that's no way to talk to a guest in our home."

"I didn't invite him to be a guest in our home."

"That's okay, Mrs. Knight." Cole laughs it off. "I actually wasn't invited. We had plans to meet at the park and since Whitney doesn't have a car right now I figured I'd swing by and get her."

"That's very thoughtful of you," my grandpa adds.

"How did you know I don't have a car?" I'm racking my brain trying to remember telling him that and I've got nothing.

He gives me a meaningful look. "You mentioned it the night we met."

"Oh." I look down and fidget with my fingers as if I'm going to be caught by my grandparents for having done something I wasn't supposed to.

Sparky, who was somewhere in the back of the house, comes trotting into the living room, his little nails clicking on the hardwood.

"This little guy is Sparky," my grandma tells Cole by way

of introduction.

"Well, hello there, Sparky." Cole smiles down at the dog.

Without missing a beat the little powder puff walks right up to Cole, sniffs his ankle, then raises up and starts humping his leg. Sparky's little hips push back and forth so fast and with so much determination it's hard not to be impressed.

"Oh, goodness," my grandma says and puts her hands over her face.

Cole is now holding his leg out to his side like he has no idea what to do and I laugh because this is probably the only time he didn't know how to handle someone who wants to bang him.

Still laughing, I lean over and snatch Sparky up off his leg. It takes the little guy a second to realize what I've done because his hips are still moving in midair until I set him back down on the floor.

"Sorry about that," I say to Cole, who seems a little uncomfortable for the first time since I met him. "Bad dog," I say to Sparky, but really who am I to scold him? I get it, Sparky. Believe me, I get it. I want to screw him, too.

"Would you mind taking him with you to the park?" my grandma asks. "He could use some fresh air. We were going to go earlier, but your grandpa wasn't feeling up to it."

"Are you okay?" I ask the man who raised me.

"Your grandma worries too much. I'm fine, sweet pea." A warm feeling permeates my chest at his use of the term of endearment he's called me my whole life.

"We'd love to take him," Cole says before I can decline.

I roll my eyes. Why is Cole pretending he's a nice guy for my grandparents' benefit? What does he care?

"Let me grab his leash," my grandma says and walks over to the front hall closet. She pulls a red leash off a hook on the inside of the door.

"I'll grab you some plastic bags for when he does his

business." My grandpa shuffles to the back of the house toward the kitchen.

Ugh. I forgot about the part of dog ownership where you have to pick up their fecal matter.

I take the leash from my grandma and bend over to put it on Sparky. His tongue is hanging out of the one side of his mouth and the excitement vibrates off of him.

Once I'm done I stand back up and look down at him with my hands on my hips. This dog is nothing but trouble. He better behave. I have enough on my mind without adding a canine companion into the mix.

"Here you go." My grandpa comes up behind me and I take the plastic bags from him and shove them into my purse.

"Thanks."

"You two have a nice time," my grandma says. "It was a pleasure meeting you, Cole."

"Same to both of you. I hope to see you again sometime." He smiles that smile that makes my insides tingle again and turns to open the door.

What the hell is he talking about? Why would he be seeing them again?

I pick up Sparky's leash and follow Cole out the door. "Bye." I turn to look at my grandparents and my grandma has a grin on her face so wide it's possible her dentures might fall out.

Ha! Forget it, Grandma. Not going to happen. This little walk today is all about etching the lines in the sand and making sure they aren't crossed.

THE RIDE OVER TO the park is silent. Well, except for Sparky's yipping whenever he sees another dog being walked by their owner. I tried to put him in the back seat, but he just kept climbing up to the front and using my lap as a perch to see out the window.

"He really likes you," Cole says, turning onto the street that I know will take us to our destination.

"He likes anyone with two feet and a heartbeat," I say.

"I'm not so sure about that. He seems pretty enamored with you specifically."

I glance over at Cole and shrug. "If you say so."

"I understand where he's coming from." His voice is soft and quiet so I'm not certain if I was supposed to hear him or not, so I pretend I don't. Because I have no idea what to do with a statement like that. And the way I'm already second-guessing what he could mean by it only tells me that I need to stay as far away from Cole as possible. Which is going to make the next eight months impossible.

Cole pulls his Jeep into the parking lot and finds a spot to park in. A Jeep. I know. I mean, it's a nice Jeep with all the fanciest features, but knowing the type of money his family has, I was really surprised that this is what he chooses to drive. I've seen his brother's sports car, which doesn't seem that practical to me in San Francisco, but it screams money. I guess I expected the same from Cole. I'll begrudgingly admit to being pleasantly surprised.

"All right, you little fur ball. You ready to do this?"

*Arf.*

I pick Sparky up and place him on the ground outside the vehicle. He immediately begins sniffing around and leading us toward the grass in the park.

"Looks like it might rain."

I follow Cole's gaze to the sky above and see that he's right. Some clouds are moving in quickly, as they tend to do here. Hopefully, the rain will hold off because I'm not sure I'll be able to work up the nerve again to do this with him.

Cole and I head to the path and walk in silence for a minute. When we stop to let Sparky do his business—just a number one, thankfully—Cole puts his hands in the front pockets of his jeans. He tilts his head like he's trying to figure me out or something and then finally speaks. "So . . . why did you want to meet up?"

"You don't remember who I am, do you?"

"Sure I do. You're that cute brunette who was lamenting her life in my bar, had one too many, and then took me home to have her way with me." His eyes sparkle and he's clearly joking with me.

"Har, har," I say and roll my eyes. "Before that."

He shakes his head slowly and I can practically see the wheels turning in his head. Did he sleep with me before? Did we work together? Go to school together?

"Don't give yourself an aneurysm trying to figure it out." Sparky's now tugging on the leash and so we start a slow walk down the path again.

In my peripheral vision, Cole shoves a hand through his hair. Damn. I would've really enjoyed having that visual in my memory bank for later.

"Should I remember you?" he asks from behind me.

I blow out an exasperated sigh and turn toward him. "Six years ago. When Tahlia and Chase started dating they tried to set us up . . . arranged for us to meet at a restaurant in China-town . . ."

I angle my head to look at him and I see genuine confusion there. Until I don't. And then all color drains from his face. "That was you?" I purse my lips and nod. His eyes widen. "Oh, shit. I swear I didn't know."

God, the idiot *still* doesn't get it.

"I'm not mentioning it because I think you should have known when you saw me." We never even met in person, so how would he? I stop and inhale a deep breath in an effort to prevent my temper from running away from me. "Do you even remember what you said to me before you hung up? While I sat alone at the table in the restaurant?" I add.

Cole hangs his head and looks genuinely concerned about what I might say. "I'm afraid to even ask."

"I was so stunned that I was being stood up that I said something stupid like, 'What about our Chinese dinner?' You responded with, 'I'm about to feast on an even better Asian buffet. I'm good.' That was followed by a girl's giggle and then you hung up." My face reddens as I recall how humiliating the entire ordeal was.

Cole shakes his head and runs his hand through his hair again. This time I catch it. And boy, was it worth catching, making me hate myself just a little because I am not supposed to be ogling this guy while I try to give him a piece of my mind.

"I really said that?"

"You did." I stop and face him, crossing my arms over my chest. To my surprise, Sparky accepts this and doesn't protest by tugging on the leash.

"Wow. I don't know what to say."

"Seriously, Cole?" I reach out and swat him on the chest. "Sorry would be a good start."

"I'm sorry," he says while laughing.

Really believable.

Pissed that he's not taking this at all seriously, I stomp forward on the path. He catches me by my elbow to get me to stop and turn to face him. I don't say anything, but I give him a look that I hope implies that if he says the wrong fucking thing I'm going to rip off his balls and feed them to him with a nice Chianti. Hannibal Lecter would be proud.

"I wasn't laughing at you." When I still don't speak, he continues. "I just can't believe I actually said that. I mean . . . who the hell did I think I was?"

Though I hate the fact that I'm being charmed by him, I give in anyway. "Hugh Hefner?"

He laughs. "Apparently."

"I sat around in that restaurant waiting and waiting. It was so embarrassing. The waiter felt so sorry for me that he told the manager and they comped the two drinks I had while I was sitting there."

Cole cringes and runs a hand down his face. "Shit."

"Yeah, shit."

I have to say . . . this Cole seems like a totally different guy than the one that was at the engagement party. *This* Cole reminds me of the guy I met that night at the Thirsty Monk. Not a totally unlikeable guy.

"I don't know what to say except apologize and tell you that I'm not that guy anymore."

I raise a brow. "Sure didn't seem that way at the engagement party."

He shifts his weight and looks down at his feet for a second before returning his gaze to my own. "You thought you had me all figured out. I didn't want to disappoint you." There's an edge to his voice and it's clear to me that I struck a nerve that night. Interesting.

"In my defence, I thought I did. When I realized who you were . . . and then the fact that I'd gone home with you a few weeks before . . ." I trail off and I'm not able to meet his eyes when I say that last part.

"You thought nothing had changed."

I shrug.

"The night you came back to my place . . . that was different."

"How?"

He pauses and then shakes his head. "Doesn't matter. Just was."

Another interesting little tidbit I file away and plan to examine later. "All of that doesn't matter anyway. I wanted to meet with you today to clear the air. You know, since we're going to have to see each other a lot in the coming months."

A small smile tugs at the corner of his mouth. "I'm glad you did."

"I also wanted to ask you not to mention anything to Tahlia about us going home together."

He raises a brow now and studies me.

"It would only stress her out more and she'd be worrying if the two of us can coexist. I don't want to add to an already stressful time for her." I keep the part about her knowing exactly how much Cole's little stunt affected my life to myself.

"She's getting married, not getting divorced," he says.

"I'm aware. But even good stress is still stress."

"If you say so."

"Look, something you need to know about Tahl is that she's been planning her wedding in her head since she was ten. This is a *big* deal for her. And her mother isn't going to get off her back until she has the perfect society wedding. You haven't mentioned anything to Chase, have you?"

Cole crinkles his forehead and shakes his head. "My personal life is none of my brother's business."

"Good. So, you agree?"

He shrugs. "I guess so. If you're comfortable lying to your friend about it."

Ouch. That stings. "It's to help her, and really what's the point in telling her? Nothing is ever going to happen again."

He chuckles for a split second. "If you say so."

That gives me pause. "I do. Why wouldn't I?"

"You think I don't notice the way you check me out every time you see me?"

I clench my hands into fists at my side. Who actually says this shit out loud? "I don't know what you're talking about."

He chuckles at me. Again. And it makes me want to rip

his larynx from his throat so I don't have to listen to it anymore.

He takes a step toward me so there's little to no room between us and I'm forced to tip my chin up to look at him. "Really? I must be imagining the way your eyes dilate every time I meet your gaze. Or the way your breath hitches just a little any time I touch you." To prove his point, he takes his index finger and runs it along the curve of my neck. I suppress a small shiver but from the shit-eating grin on his face I can tell that he knows he's affected me. "Maybe I'm dreaming up the way your nipples harden whenever I get within a few inches of you." His gaze slips down to my chest and I don't need to follow it to know that he's right.

"It's a little chilly out here," I say meekly in defence.

"Admit it." He leans in even further and I can smell his cologne and feel his breath tickle my cheek. His mouth is now lined up beside my ear when he says, "You want me."

I push at his chest and roll my eyes. "You really do have the world's biggest ego."

"You told me I had the world's biggest cock the night you came home with me."

Heat floods my face because I can't even defend myself. I was too drunk to remember. "I think you've got that twisted. I probably told you you *were* the world's biggest dick. And look at that, I'm right."

He looks like he's about to say some quip when he pauses and studies me for a few beats. "Wait a minute. You really don't remember saying that, do you?"

Shit. I do not want him to know that I don't recall what happened that night. It will only give him the advantage. "Come on, Sparky." I turn and begin walking further down the path. Sparky's loyal because although I know he's as attracted to Cole as I am (based on the two-pump hump on his leg when they first met), he follows me and prances happily by my side.

At first, I think that Cole's going to let us walk away, but he catches up after a few seconds.

"Do you remember anything from that night?"

"I remember you feeding me drinks at the bar so I'd go home with you."

"Whoa. Hold up." He grabs my elbow and forces me to stop once again and look at him. "I was not getting you drunk to take you home. You were already well on your way to being shit-faced before I even stepped into the bar that night." I stay silent because it's true and I have no retaliation to that. "I had a few myself, if you recall. It was your idea to leave the bar together. I did not take advantage of you."

I can't believe I'm about to ask this, but I have to know. I suck in a big breath and swallow my pride. "What happened after we got to your place?"

A lopsided smirk pulls up one corner of his mouth. "You don't remember anything?" I shake my head. "Interesting."

That's all he says. Interesting. And I'm left looking at him, waiting for him to enlighten me. "Are you going to tell me?"

"Nah. I think I'll keep that to myself because I, for one, remember *everything*."

The way he says everything has me clenching my thighs together. The word sounds about as loaded as I was that night, which is a lot.

"Seriously. You're not going to tell me?"

He waits a beat before answering. "I tell you what. I'll reveal one thing that happened that night every time I see you *if* you give me a chance and don't act like a total bitch."

"I am not a bitch." I cross my arms over my chest.

"I didn't say you *are* one. I said you can't *act* like one. There's a difference."

"Semantics."

"Specifics."

I stand there heated and staring at him. I'm equal parts angry and hot for the guy, which is messing with my mind.

"Do we have a deal?"

"Fine."

He holds out his hand and I take it. We shake on it and I let go pretending my palm isn't still tingling from his touch.

"Good. And to show you I'm a man of my word I'll even fill you in on something right now even though you haven't been especially nice to me this afternoon."

I grit my teeth and clench my fists, otherwise I'm afraid I might actually haul off and hit the guy.

He reaches into the inside pocket of his jacket. "You forgot this at my house."

It all happens in slow motion. His hand pulls out of his jacket and I see a flash of bright pink. As he pushes it closer to me I realize it's the Tickled Pink vibrator that Lennon gave me.

My breath hitches, my heart stutters, and my hands fly up to cover my face. He's holding it out in between us like he's passing me some mundane object and before I know what's happening Sparky jumps up and snatches it from his hand.

And because I'm so brilliant and dropped the leash to cover my face, he takes off in the direction of the small forest at break-neck speed, hot pink vibrator clenched tightly between his teeth.

"Shit!" I yell and start to run after him. It's only seconds before Cole overtakes me and is running ahead of me.

Sparky really knows how to work those little legs of his. I had no idea he could run this fast. When he reaches the edge of the forest he stops and turns to face us. I swear the little shit is grinning at me with that sex toy between his teeth. I can't focus on the complete mortification of having Cole return the vibrator to me because if I return home without this little fur ball my grandma is going to kill me.

Cole and I both slow our approach and try to come at the

powder puff like you'd approach a wild animal.

"Come here, Sparky," I say in a soft and lilting voice. "Come over here." I stretch my hand out and for a second I think that maybe he's going to make this easy on me and head my way.

Thunder claps from above us and Sparky darts further into the park.

"Damn it." We both follow him and within seconds the sky opens up and cold rain starts pelting down on us. This situation just got a whole lot shittier, given the fact that I chose to wear a white shirt today.

"Sparky!" I yell after him.

"Come here, boy!" Cole calls out. I roll my eyes at that one. Does that even work?

Sparky comes to a grouping of trees and seems unsure what to do. Thunder sounds from the black clouds hanging overhead and Sparky panics again, whipping his head side to side, looking for a place to go.

I see it at the same time he does. A downed tree that's hollow inside. He turns and covers the few feet to the entrance in seconds.

"Sparky, no!"

But it's too late. He's already inside.

"Shit. Now what are we going to do?" I scream and stomp my foot on the ground like a two-year-old.

I glance over at Cole, who's kneeled at the other end of the log, peering into it. "Hey, buddy."

I begin to shiver as my wet clothes cling to my body. Lightning flashes and I wrap my arms around myself in an effort to conserve body heat. "This is all your fault, you know."

"How is this my fault?" He raises his head and glares at me.

"If you hadn't held out that . . . thing like a bone, he never would have gone after it. I mean, who does that in the middle of a public park?"

"Who leaves their vibrator in someone else's house?"

"It's not *my* vibrator."

He screws his face up. "So, you walk around with other people's sex toys?"

"Yes. No!" I let out some noise that's a mix of a scream and frustration. "You can be so annoying."

He ignores my last comment. "Well, which is it, yes or no?"

"Technically yes. But it's brand new and a friend had just given it to me to try out."

Cole shakes his head to himself. "I swear I'll never understand women."

I blow out a long breath. "Can we just focus on getting Sparky back so that we can get the hell out of here?" I cast him an irritated look and bend back down on my haunches and peer into the hole from the other side. Sparky's still there, cowering against the inside of the large log, hot pink vibrator still in his mouth like it's a fucking stick.

"Come here, Sparky. Here, boy."

Sparky doesn't move but just continues to stare straight ahead at me.

"Come here," I say in my most cajoling voice when all I really want to do is scream, *Get out here, you little runt. I'm soaked and freezing my ass off and you're running around the park with a pink vibrator in front of this insanely hot guy who probably already thinks I'm nuts.*

But Sparky doesn't move.

In frustration, I stand and stomp my foot again. "He's never coming out of there."

"Let me try." Cole comes over to my side so I take a step back to allow him room. He bends down in front of me and I have to admit that the view isn't half bad.

"Sparky. Sparky, come here." He slowly reaches his hand forward and into the opening of the log for Sparky to smell. I can't see if it's working or not, but Cole holds his pose for a minute and then I see Sparky's little face near the opening.

I guess Cole's scent is truly irresistible. Even to another species.

He moves his hand just outside of the opening now. "Come here, boy. You know you want to."

*Boy, do I.*

Sparky moves a couple more inches until his entire face is out of the log. I hold my breath hoping he won't retreat. Cole moves his hands closer and closer until they're wrapped around Sparky's little body and he's lifting him to his chest.

"There, little guy. That wasn't so bad, was it?" he says as he pats his head. "Do you want to get out of here?" Cole glances over at me and I come out of the trance I was in watching him be so gentle to the little minx.

"Oh. Yeah, of course."

He closes the distance between us. "We don't have to, you know. A forest fuck in the rain could be kind of cool." His gaze flicks down to my shirt, which is white, soaked, and plastered to my chest. I don't have to look down to know that my nipples are erect and proudly on display.

"Yeah, not happening."

"You sure about that?" he says. He bends to the side to put Sparky on the ground and closes those final few inches between us until our chests are just barely touching.

"Nothing can ever happen between us again." Jeez, even I can tell I didn't mean that by the sound of my voice.

"I would have thought with the way you were crying out my name last time that you'd want a repeat."

I still. "What do you mean?"

He slowly shakes his head back and forth. "Don't you remember our deal? You have to be nice to me and I'll tell you next time I see you."

Damn it. I'd give almost anything to be able to remember that night now. If I was begging whatever was going on must have been damn good.

"Fine." I rip the leash from his hand and begin to walk back out of the forest. "It doesn't matter anyway."

I hear Cole following on the forest floor behind me. "Sure it does. I know as well as you do that you're dying to know."

I simply shrug. It's useless. He's obviously enjoying playing this little game with me and I'm not going to give him the satisfaction of knowing for sure how much it's bugging me that he's the only one who remembers what happened that night.

Cole jogs up until he's beside me. "You keep forgetting this."

In his hand is the Tickled Pink vibrator. Without a word, I snatch it from his hand and continue walking with my head held high and long confident strides I don't really feel.

I'm amazed that I didn't give any thought to the fact that I left it there. I can only assume my subconscious either thought he was too much of a gentleman to bring it up or it was blocking it out completely as a way of coping. Clearly assumption number one was wrong. There's nothing gentlemanly about Cole Webber.

Sadly, I seem to kind of like it that way.

# chapter

# ELEVEN

*I* HAVE TO NAIL him.

*This.* Not him. I have to nail this interview.

Cole's been on my mind ever since that day at the park last week and apparently, he still is. I can't believe he's even coming to mind while I'm sitting in the reception area waiting to be interviewed for my dream job.

WHFI is a Bay area station and they're looking for someone to do their on-air weekly investigative report. Even though I worked at a newspaper before, this was always my end game. The chance to be on air doesn't come around often and to be able to do it while investigating and righting wrongs for the less fortunate? It doesn't get any better than that. At least not for me.

"Miss Knight?" I glance up at the receptionist across the room sitting at her desk. "They're running a little behind on the interviews, so it will be a few more minutes."

"No problem." I smile wide. My old boss at the paper used to tell me that he'd always check with the receptionist to see what her impression of each interviewee was, since everyone's on their best behavior when they're in front of the person who has the ability to give you your paycheck. It's how they treat the people who can't do anything for them that's the best judge of their character.

I sit there letting my one knee bounce up and down for a minute when an attractive blonde enters, goes to speak with the receptionist, and then comes to sit down near me.

I try to glance over at her inconspicuously so I can size up my competition and then wish I hadn't. If I'm up against her I'm in trouble. She's gorgeous. Actually, she's beyond gorgeous. If I'm honest, she reminds me of Kate Upton.

Look, it's not that I have zero self-esteem, because I like to think that I have a decent amount. But if we're comparing apples to apples and one of those apples is just your regular average apple and the other is juicy, shiny, and would win the prize for best apple at the spring fair then they always pick the latter. Being on air is about being able to do the job *and* being attractive. Sad? Maybe. But that's the reality of it. The station owners aren't going to put Quasimodo on the evening news.

A little piece of my confidence shreds away and falls to the floor.

"Are you here for an interview, too?"

It takes me a second to realize that she's talking to me.

"You look nervous." She smiles and Jesus, she's even more radiant. A part of me wants to dislike her because she's probably going to win this job over me, but there's something sweet about her.

"I am. And I am. Nervous, that is."

"Me, too."

"Are you interviewing, too?" I ask, hoping she says no.

She nods her head and my stomach twists. "I'm hoping for the sportscaster job."

Suddenly a ray of hope shines through the dark, desolate sky. "Well, good luck." And I mean it because she seems nice.

"I'm here for the reporter job."

That awkward silence ensues for a moment. You know, the one where you're chatting with someone you don't really know and you're not sure whether to continue the conversation or just let it drop. "So, you're big into sports?" I ask.

"I grew up with four older brothers so I didn't have much choice." She hesitates and seems to consider whether to divulge the rest of her story for a moment. "I know I don't look like your typical sports reporter."

I'm not sure what to say to that because she's right. "No, you don't. They usually have more chest hair. Less chest." I decide to go with stating the obvious.

"Right?" She laughs. "I've been cursed with these things since I was a teenager." She looks down at her very, very ample bosom.

"Really? I was praying for something like that when I was a teenager."

We laugh together this time and she sticks out her hand to shake mine. "I'm Kelsey."

I take her hand. "I'm Whitney."

"Nice to meet you." She smiles but then slumps back into her chair a bit. "It's been so hard trying to get a job in this industry with these. No one wants to take me seriously, but I know what I'm doing. I've been watching sports since I was in the womb and I went to broadcasting school. I can do the job. I just need someone to take a shot on me."

"That has to be frustrating." I feel bad for Kelsey. She seems nice and though I was wishing I could have a figure like hers when I first saw her, now I'm wondering if it's more curse than blessing.

"Can you believe that one station head down near Los Angeles actually told me I wouldn't be able to do the job? That these"—she points to her considerable assets—"would be too distracting for the players."

"He actually said that?" I see a spark in her eyes and though she comes across as sweet and fairly innocent it's clear that she can hold her own when provoked.

"Out loud."

"Wow. I don't even have words for that." My phone buzzes from my purse on my lap and I reach in to find it. "Excuse me for a second."

Kelsey nods.

My heart picks up pace a bit when I see it's a text from Cole.

*Cole: Hey. Just talked to Chase. Wedding duty calls.*

*Me: I'm sitting waiting to go into an interview. What's up?*

*Cole: That's what she said.*

*Me: Seriously?*

*Cole: You've never seen The Office?*

*Me: Of course I've seen it. What I mean is that I'm kinda busy so get on with it.*

*Cole: That's what she said.*

*Me: I'm turning my phone off now.*

*Cole: Hold up. Okay, I talked to Chase and we're on deck.*

*Me: For what?*

*Cole: Meet me at the bar and I'll fill you in.*

*Me: That's what he said.*

*Cole: Now who's wasting time?*

*Me: I'll be over when I'm done.*

*Cole: I'll still be here.*

*Me: K, see you then.*

I power my phone off so that it won't disturb my interview and toss it back into my purse.

"Sorry about that," I say to Kelsey.

"No problem. Boyfriend?"

"Oh, God, no. Annoying best man of a wedding that I'm in."

Kelsey grins and leans forward like she's about to share a secret. "There must be something good about him if he's putting that smile on your face."

Before I can deny her claim the woman behind the desk interrupts us.

"Miss Knight?" the reception says. "Mr. Jeffries will see you now."

My stomach does another somersault as the nerves return. I'd almost forgotten about them while I was out here chatting with Kelsey.

"Good luck," she says and I stand from my chair.

"Thank you. And same to you."

She smiles and I follow the aging receptionist through a cubicle laden office bustling with people until we reach a corner office. It's sparsely decorated and not that huge, but it's clear someone of importance resides here. It overlooks the city with a wall made of glass and there's a wooden shelving unit with a bunch of different awards on it against one wall.

A well-groomed man in his mid-forties with slicked-back hair and a lilac dress shirt with matching tie sits behind the impressive desk.

"Mr. Jeffries, this is Whitney Knight. Your three-thirty."

"Thanks, Margo."

She gives me a small smile before closing door behind her when she leaves.

"Please have a seat." Mr. Jeffries gestures to one of the leather chairs across from his desk. "It's good to meet you. Sorry about running behind." He leans over his desk with his hand extended and I take the offering, giving him a firm handshake.

"It's a pleasure to meet you, sir."

He opens a file folder in front of him and pulls out a few sheets of paper stapled together, which I recognize as my résumé. "It says here you were let go from your last job at the *Sacramento Chronicle*?" He turns his attention to me, but unlike a few of the other interviews I've gone to, I see no judgment there, only curiosity.

"They were downsizing and I didn't make the cut. I was lower on the seniority scale than most of the other people there." I could add that it wasn't that that resulted in me being let go, but I don't. Because I want this job.

"Things are pretty lean in the print industry right now. It's tough to sell ad space when everyone's moving to free online sources to gather their news."

I don't respond because he turns his attention back to my résumé. "What did you find the most challenging part of your position at the paper?"

From there we launch into a rather enjoyable conversation about my experience and why I want the job of an investigative reporter. I'm hoping my passion for uncovering the truth and helping those who can't help themselves shines through. Overall, I'm feeling confident by the time we're wrapping up.

Mr. Jeffries glances at his watch. "I've enjoyed talking with you, Whitney, but I have to wrap this up. I have one more interview and then my husband is dragging me to the 49ers game."

I smile. At least if I get the job I won't have to worry about *this* boss trying to seduce me. "Not a big football fan, are you?"

He grimaces. "Not at all. I don't know why I let him drag me to these things, but he's a sports nut, so what can I do?

Relationships are all about compromise."

I rise from my seat and reach out to shake his head. "It was a pleasure meeting you, sir. I hope I hear from you soon."

"Someone from WHFI will be in touch. I remember what it was like when I was out looking for a job. It's the worst not hearing anything back."

I exhale in relief. "Thank you. I appreciate that. It really is the worst not knowing either way."

"Excellent. We'll talk soon then." He nods.

"Enjoy the game," I say with a little cheek.

He laughs and picks up his phone and I can hear him asking the receptionist to send in the next interviewee. When I pass Kelsey in the hall I wink at her and mouth, *Good luck.* Regardless of what happens with me, she seems like good people and I hope she gets the job.

As I enter the elevator to make my way down to street level I send a small prayer up to whoever is listening to help me get this job.

With that taken care of I mentally shift to my next task—meet with Cole. Without succumbing to his charm. That's always so much easier said than done.

*chapter*

# TWELVE

*I* ARRIVE AT THE Thirsty Monk and when I walk through the door and smell the stale beer and fried food it reminds me of the night I met Cole. I still don't recall what happened when we went back to his house. But damn, do I wish I did. It's disconcerting to think that Cole knows something about me that I don't. I've always relied on myself and I don't relish having to rely on him to tell me what went down that night.

I glance around and there are a few patrons scattered at various tables around the place, but no Cole. I walk over to take a seat at the bar, the same seat as the night we met.

The pretty blonde bartender smiles at me and comes over. "What can I get yah?"

"I'm looking for Cole. Is he around?"

Her forehead crinkles just a little bit and she gives me a quick once-over before she manages to put the smile back on her face. "He's in the back. Can I tell him who's here?"

"It's Whitney. I think he's expecting me." I smile back at her, but I know it's strained because this girl is giving me the vibe that I'm invading her territory and it makes me wonder what the deal is with the two of them.

She doesn't say anything else before she leaves.

A minute later Cole comes out from the back, dressed in a pair of worn jeans and a gray t-shirt with a logo that says Hard Rock Whiskey over the top of his pecs. The cotton hugs every sharp line of the muscles in his arms and chest. He smiles wide at me and it makes his eyes kind of sparkle and it has me briefly wondering if they look like that for everyone or just when he sees me.

Which is something that I should absolutely not be wondering, because he's off limits.

"Hey, you want to grab a table over there?" He gestures to a table near the window that doesn't have any other patrons around it.

"Sure," I say and slip off the bar stool.

The blonde girl returns to her post behind the bar, but she's eyeing the two of us warily like she's trying to figure us out.

"Do you want anything to drink?" Cole asks once we're seated.

"Maybe just a water."

He raises a brow. "No whiskey?"

I roll my eyes. "I think I'm safer around you if I stick to non-alcoholic beverages."

He chuckles. "Let's be honest. Even sober you find me irresistible."

I laugh and shake my head at him. "I think you're mixing that up. It's the other way around."

Instead of delivering some quick quip back like I expected he looks me straight in the eye and says in a low, serious voice, "That goes without saying."

We hold one another's gaze for a minute before I clear my throat and look away. The pull between us is magnetic and hard to resist. But, I remind myself, I have to. I know the type of man Cole is and he'd take my heart, fill it up, and then burst it into a million pieces while I sat there willingly and let him do it.

I've always prided myself on standing on my own two feet and this man would bring me to my knees.

After an awkward silence, I ask, "So what did you call me over for?"

He shrugs. "Maybe I just wanted to see you."

I ignore the thrill that zips through me because I'm sure he's just messing with me. "Can you be serious for a second?" I ask with an exasperated sigh.

"Chase and Tahlia want us to scope out a bunch of places for them to have the ceremony and report back."

"Are you serious?" I scrunch my face up.

Cole shrugs. "He called me and that's what he said."

"Isn't that really something the bride and groom should do?"

"I don't think we're picking it, we just need to figure out the best options so they can spend their limited time looking at those."

"I'm still in disbelief that Tahlia wouldn't want to do all this on her own. I need to call her."

"You really think I'm making this shit up?" Cole asks in an annoyed voice.

"Relax. Just let me call her." I grab my phone from my purse and pull up Tahl's contact info then hit the little green button to call her.

"Yeah?" she answers, sounding rushed.

"Hey, Tahl. It's me. I was just talking to Cole and he was telling me that you and Chase want us to vet some places for the ceremony."

"Yes, sorry. I've been meaning to call you all day, but work has been crazy and I had to run home and pack. To the airport, please," she says to someone else. I hear a car door slam a second later and realize she must have just gotten into a cab.

"Everything okay?"

"Just a small crisis at one of the plants out of state. I have to go work my magic."

"All right then. I'm happy to help. I just wanted to hear it from you." I purse my lips in concern for my friend.

"Thanks, Whit. I'll text you a list of places to check out as soon as I'm through security and waiting at the gate, okay?"

"For sure. I'm surprised you're not getting married in a church."

"We were both raised on capitalism, not Catholicism." She gives a rueful laugh. "We've decided to go with a non-denominational venue. I'm swamped here at work this week and I know you have a little extra time on your hands . . ." She pauses because I know she feels bad saying it, but it's the truth. "From what Chase says Cole doesn't take work too seriously, so I'm sure he wouldn't mind driving you around."

"Okay, if that's what you want."

"Just take lots of pictures. And Whit?"

"Yeah?"

"You're the best."

Any trepidation I have about roaming the city side by side with Cole eases at the warmth of her voice. I know she's under a lot of pressure at work and I do have the time to help her out. I want her day to be exactly what she envisions and anything to help her achieve that, I'll do.

I hit end on the call and look across to Cole. "Well, this should be interesting."

The sly grin that pulls up one corner of his mouth tells me that interesting is probably the least of what the next couple of days will be.

*chapter*

# THIRTEEN

"WHAT'S NEXT ON THE list?" Cole asks me from the driver's seat of his Jeep.

I scroll through my notes on my phone. "Bluxome Street Winery," I say. "Fifty-three Bluxome Street."

Cole punches the address into his phone and follows the directions of the annoying computer lady. I wonder if he knows that you can change the setting so that it'll sound like a hot Australian guy?

This is our third stop today. The first two places were busts and nowhere near regal or posh enough for Tahlia and Chase. I'm starting to understand why they stuck us with handling all the runaround for them. This endeavor is seriously labor-intensive.

We find parking on the street and make our way over to a very industrial-looking building. It's clean and modern, but I'm still surprised this was on Tahlia's list. Tahl is more what I would call a traditionalist and I don't see much here that I think would appeal to her.

We step inside and the place is essentially one big open-space warehouse with super-high ceilings. The rafters are wrapped in twinkle lights and at the far end of the room are shelves filled with wooden barrels, presumably of wine. Industrial lights encased with round glass hang from the ceiling, giving a trendy vibe rather than that of a run-down warehouse.

"Are you Whitney and Cole?" An attractive woman in her mid-twenties approaches us from a doorway I didn't notice on the left. She smiles at us both and I don't miss the way her eyes linger a little longer on Cole.

Can't say I blame her. He's wearing dark denim today, hiking boots, and a flannel shirt with the sleeves rolled up. Oh, and he's let his beard grow in a little more than normal so he's giving off this rough-and-tumble, woodsy outdoorsman vibe.

Not that I've given it much thought or anything.

"You must be Claudia?" I ask, remembering the name of the woman we'd be meeting from the notes in my phone.

"That's me." She shakes both our hands when she reaches us. "I spoke with Tahlia earlier this week and she said to expect the both of you. I handle all the event bookings here."

"It's nice to meet you," Cole says and smiles in a friendly way.

I can tell that Claudia is charmed by him and I immediately divert all our attention back to the reason we're here.

"Would you be able to show us around and explain how the ceremony would be run here?" I ask.

She blinks a couple of times—catching herself, I think—then smiles. "Of course. Follow me."

"Do you mind if I take pictures to send to Tahlia?" I ask.

"I'd like to take some as well if you don't mind," Cole says.

"Of course not." She turns and starts walking toward the back of the warehouse and we both follow. "I have a book back here with pictures in it of some of the various events we've hosted here. It will give you an idea of how well we can transform the space depending on what vibe the bride and groom are going for."

We all gather around a large photo album on one of the tables. Claudia points out some of the various options different weddings have chosen to use.

"Do you have a brochure I could take with us?" Cole asks.

"I'll be sure to get you one before you leave." She pats his shoulder and he smiles over at her.

I'm beginning to feel like the third wheel.

For the next half an hour Claudia tries to sell us on the space and how perfect it would be for a Webber wedding. The place is lovely, but I'm not really getting the feeling that this is what Tahlia has in mind. I haven't had to do much talking because Cole has suddenly become Chatty Cathy, asking all kinds of questions and showing a real interest in the place.

He had next to nothing to say at all the other places and suddenly he can't keep his trap shut. What gives? Is it the set of double D's on Claudia that were missing from our first two stops?

"How many people can you fit in here for a ceremony?" he asks.

"Approximately a hundred and fifty seated and three hundred standing."

He rubs at the stubble on his jaw with one hand. It's the most mundane of actions but the throbbing in my nether regions has me shifting my weight. "I doubt this will be big enough for what they have in mind," he says more to himself. I'm still admiring his movements when he directs his attention over to me. "Any idea how many guests they're inviting?"

I copy Claudia's earlier actions and blink myself out of the trance I'm in before I can respond. "Um . . . no. I forgot to ask."

"Okay, well, we'll report back to my brother and his fiancée and they can figure it out from there. Thanks so much for your time today, Claudia."

She blushes when he takes her hand in his and shakes it.

"The pleasure was all mine."

I'm sure there's an invitation there based on her sultry tone, but Cole doesn't seem to notice, casually putting his hands into his front pockets while I say my goodbye to our eager hostess.

We're silent as we make our way back to his Jeep. Once we're inside and I've given him the address of our next stop I decide to just voice what I'm thinking in my head.

"You seemed very interested in there. I don't think you spoke more than five sentences at the first couple of places. What gives?"

He glances over at me for a second before returning his attention back to the road. "I like how they've been able to come up with another stream of income to offset the costs of their primary business, that's all." He shrugs, dismissing my curiosity, but I know. I just know there's more to it. "Do you want to grab something to eat after this next one? I'm starved," he says.

"Sure." I lean back in my seat, deciding to let the subject go for now. I'll get to the bottom of it though. I don't want to be an investigative reporter for nothing.

*chapter*

# FOURTEEN

*C*OLE AND I STEP up the staircase in front of the Bentley Reserve building and a giddy excitement invades my stomach. This place feels very much like something my friend might want for her big day. The building is an old bank built in the early 1920's and as we enter I take in the soaring hall, travertine walls, and Italian marble floors. We both stop in place and use the moment to take in the picturesque view.

"Tahlia wasn't able to get a hold of the events coordinator here, so we're just going to have to see if they'll show us around," I say.

He nods and we take a few more steps forward, the sound of our shoes echoing off the floors and the thirty-something foot ceiling above.

An older gentleman dressed in a navy suit approaches us immediately. "Can I help you?" His chin is raised and he gives off an aura of sophistication and snobbery. As if the two of us are not good enough to be here.

True, we're not dressed as nicely as he is, but that's no reason for him to give us attitude.

"We're here to check out the venue for a wedding," I say.

The man makes a show of taking me in from top to bottom and then does the same to Cole. I guess he doesn't find the lumbersexual look as appealing as it is to me. "The price list is online. You might want to look at that first. I'm not sure you'll find it . . . suitable."

My cheeks heat and I clench my fists at my side, wanting so badly to give this man a piece of my mind, but knowing I can't screw this up for Tahlia. I open my mouth to speak, but before I can say a word Cole's large hand takes mine. He pries open my fingers and intertwines them with his own. Heat radiates up my arm and I look over at him, my eyes wide.

"I can assure you, Mr . . ." Cole lets it hang there until the man is forced to answer.

"Berkshire." He says it with such superiority that I want to slap the smug look off his face.

"I can assure you, Mr. Berkshire, that money is no object for my fiancée and I." Cole squeezes my hand and looks over at me and then winks with the eye that the other man can't see.

I smile back, intrigued by this game he's playing, but more than willing to participate if it means making this jerk in front of us feel as small as he made me feel.

Mr. Berkshire clasps his hands in front of him. "All the same, you should look online first, and then if you find it within your means you can call to book an appointment with me. We don't take walk-ins."

"I tried to call several times to book an appointment," I say.

The man's eyes narrow the tiniest amount. "Yes, well, we've been having some trouble with our voicemail system as of late."

"That's too bad. I'm sure hosting a Webber wedding would have been quite the coup for your establishment," Cole says. "Come on, sweetheart, let's go find something else." Cole drops my hand and places his own on the small of my back to lead me out of the building, but we're stopped when the dickhead makes the connection.

"Webber? As in the real-estate and restaurant Webbers?"

"The one and only," Cole says. If I didn't already know him, I would find the air of supremacy around him believable. It's fascinating how easily he's able to change his persona. "I'm Chase Webber and this is my fiancée Tahlia Santora."

Mr. Berkshire's face flames scarlet and he gives us a hesitant smile. Serves him right. "Oh, please do forgive me. I had no idea." He clasps his hands together in front of him. "We have so many couples wander in here without bothering to check out the pricing. I'm sure you can understand that we can't afford to devote our time to tire-kickers when we have much more distinguished guests such as yourself to attend to."

"See that it doesn't happen again," I say, taking my turn at this rich bitch thing. It's kind of fun.

"Of course not," Mr. Berkshire says. "Can I show you around the space and answer any questions you might have?"

Cole and I look at each other and pretend we're mulling it over for a second before he nods. "I suppose we'd still like to see what you have to offer."

"Very good," Mr. Berkshire says with a nod before turning on his heel. "Right this way."

What follows is a very in-depth tour of the place and though I'm not fond of the man in charge, I really think Tahlia will love how regal this place is. Cole continues to act like we're the happy couple—either holding my hand or with his arm around my waist the entire time we're checking the place out. It feels natural and it's easy to slip into the role of Cole's fiancée. So much so that I have to remind myself not to get too carried away.

As we finish up it seems that Mr. Berkshire may have saved the best for last. He motions behind us. "For the ceremony, Tahlia, you can make quite the dramatic entrance down our grand marble-and-steel staircase." He's smiling and he should be, because I can totally envision Tahlia in a large ballroom wedding gown inching her way down the stairs while all the guests look on from below.

A slow smile creeps across my face and Cole squeezes my hip with the arm he has slung around my waist, drawing me from my revelry.

"What do you think, sweetheart?"

I lock gazes with him. "I think it might be perfect," I say in a gentle voice.

"Why don't you head to the top of the staircase and see what your entrance will be like?"

"Oh, that's okay. I can picture it and it's lovely."

"You should give it a try," Cole urges.

"I insist," Mr. Berkshire says. He steps forward and takes my hand, leading me to the bottom of the steps. "Head on up and pretend it's your big day."

I nod and take the many steps up to the top of the grand structure.

"Now, picture yourself in your wedding gown. Music is playing announcing your big entrance. The man of your dreams is waiting for you to make him the luckiest man in the world."

I close my eyes briefly and do as he says. Instinctively I position my hands in front of me as if I'm clutching a bouquet of flowers.

"Now, take the stairs slowly, one at a time."

I open my eyes and do as he says. My eyes are trained on Cole the entire time. Each step brings me closer to him and his gaze doesn't waver either. Step by step I near him and the closer I get the stronger the connection between us feels. The imaginary swish of a wedding dress sounds each time I step down, I smell the pretend scent of the flowers I'm not carrying, and I can almost hear the classical music playing in the background.

I have bought into this fairy tale one hundred percent.

By the time I reach the final step Cole's hazel eyes are blazing and I can't look away.

We remain there, staring at each other, until our tour guide clears his throat. I blink a couple of times and then turn my attention back to the older gentleman.

It's so easy to get caught up in this with Cole and forget that this is not real. *We* are not the happy couple and I'd do well to remind myself of that.

I blink a couple of times and let my hands drop before I take up my position beside Cole again.

"How many guests can you accommodate?" Cole asks in an authoritative voice that belies the moment we just shared.

"Up to three hundred and fifty."

"Perfect," Cole responds.

There's silence then as the two of us glance around the place again, committing it to memory. I pull out my phone to take a few candid shots for Tahl.

Without warning, my stomach growls and I swear the sound echoes throughout the cavernous room, bouncing off the walls and reverberating so that it's too loud to pretend it didn't just happen. I place my hand over my stomach, but it's too late. Cole is already chuckling beside me.

"We'd better be going. It seems my fiancée needs to be fed."

My cheeks heat, but I ignore it and try to continue to play the high-society bride-to-be. "Thank you for taking the time to show us around." I extend my hand and shake Mr. Berkshire's and then Cole does the same.

The older man walks us to the exit and holds the door open for us. "Before you go, if I may be so bold as to say so . . ." Cole nods at him and he continues. "I see a lot of couples come through these doors and it's clear to me that you two are the real deal. I can always tell by the way the bride and groom look at one another. It's always in the eyes." He taps his temple with his index finger. "Congratulations on your upcoming marriage. I know you'll spend many happy years together."

Cole shifts on his feet for a second and mumbles out a thank you before leading me down the many steps at the front of the building.

Hmm. Maybe I don't dislike Mr. Berkshire as much as I thought. Then again, he's probably just blowing smoke up our asses to try to land us as clients.

Still, as I walk away holding Cole's hand I can't help but wonder which it was—truth or lie?

And that's when I realize that the bigger problem is that I actually care about the answer.

*chapter*

# FIFTEEN

OLE INSISTS ON FEEDING me before dropping me back off at home and so we each grab a sandwich from a take-out spot and he drives us to the top of Twin Peaks, an elevation that sits almost in the center of the city, to take in the view. We sit on one of the rock walls looking out over the city, our feet dangling below us.

It's the first time in a long time that I've felt at peace . . . content.

"My grandparents used to take me up here all the time when I was a little girl." I smile, reliving the memories in my mind, and then take another bite of my sandwich.

"I've always liked it up here," Cole says. "Well, when it's not the middle of tourist season."

We both laugh because it's so true. If it were in the middle of summer this place would be crawling with people and you'd be lucky to find a spot along the edge to see the view of the city. But since it's fall there's only a scattering of people here. Well, at least until the next tour bus comes by.

We eat in silence for a few minutes, but Cole keeps glancing over at me.

"Just ask."

"What?" he says, feigning ignorance.

"I can tell there's something you want to say. Just say it."

He purses his lips together for a moment. "You seem very close with your grandparents."

Immediately I know what he's getting at and I decide to save him from coming right out and asking. "My grandparents raised me."

"Oh," he says. I hear the unanswered questions he's too afraid to ask and I feel the need to explain.

"My mom isn't in my life. Hasn't been since I was an infant and she left me with her parents then never returned." I put my sandwich down to the side of me, quickly losing my appetite as the sting of that rejection bites into my chest. After all these years, you'd think I'd be used to it.

Cole reaches a hand out and places it over the top of the one I have sitting in my lap, giving it a small squeeze. "I'm sorry. That's tough."

I shrug. "I was lucky really. Rather than being stuck in some orphanage or foster home I had family to go to. My grandparents are amazing. I owe them so much."

"What about your dad?" There's hesitancy in his tone, but there's no sense in hiding anything now.

"I don't know who my dad is. My grandma told me once that she wasn't even sure if my mom ever knew. I guess she was quite the free spirit."

"So that's why you share the same last name as your grandparents . . ."

"You picked up on that, did you?" I'm impressed. Most people don't even give it any thought that I have the same last name as my mother's parents.

"Not at the time. I'd just assumed they were your dad's parents."

I shrug. "Hard to take the name of someone when you don't even know who they are."

He's quiet after that, reflective. I shift my positioning and swing my legs back and forth, waiting for him to say something.

"It couldn't have been easy growing up without your parents in your life." His voice is filled with so much sympathy that it pierces a layer of my hardened heart. Which is ridiculous, because this is not news to me. It's something I've lived with and thought I'd made peace with decades ago.

I swallow past the growing lump in my throat before I answer. "I've never known any different," I say, trying to play my emotions off.

Cole shifts his body so that he's straddling the low concrete barrier we're sitting on. He's facing me now. God, he's gorgeous. Like we're magnets drawn to each other, my own body angles to his in response.

He reaches forward and clasps both my hands in one of his. His other hand cups the side of my head, his thumb tracing a slow path back and forth across my cheek.

I close my eyes for a moment and when I open them Cole is only a few inches away. His hazel eyes are locked on mine and my heart picks up pace. When he drops his forehead to mine my fingers itch with the need to touch him and so I do. Slowly I reach forward and place my hands on his hard pecs. His muscles flex under my touch and Cole lets out a short burst of air as if in relief. It fans over my face and I become more aware of his scent. Yes, it's partly the masculine cologne he wears, but it's also in a lot of ways just him. His own natural scent and I realize for the first time how addicted I've become to it.

"Just because you don't know what you're missing doesn't

mean it didn't leave any scars," he says in a soft voice.

Tears pool in my eyes, but I refuse to shed them. I don't know why I'm letting myself get so worked up. I feel safe and free to be vulnerable with Cole and vulnerable is something I don't do.

"Whitney, where are your scars?" Both his hands thread through my hair, holding me to him.

"Whit," I practically whisper.

"What?"

"You can call me Whit now."

He groans like I've just granted him everything he ever needed and without warning, he brings his lips to mine. His tongue traces a path along the part of my lips and, unable to resist, I open to him. Our tongues slide and my breath hitches, stalling out somewhere between my chest and my throat. The slow exploring kiss soon turns hot from our undying need to quench the thirst that's been brewing.

He releases my hands and cups my cheeks with his palms. I let my hands roam from his pecs to his strong back. His fingers weave through my hair making a tight fist. Cole's teeth nip at my bottom lip before his tongue slides back into my waiting mouth.

Fireworks explode in my veins and the incessant throbbing between my legs demands to be sated. The kiss is so euphoric, Cole is throwing all the baggage I carry over the edge of this peak. If there was a bed and a mattress handy I'd allow him to strap me to the headboard to see what those lips can really do. No questions asked. No thoughts about the aftermath.

When Cole finally pulls away his hands are still in my hair and we sit there, both of our chests heaving while we try to gather air into our lungs. Our gazes take each other in.

"Where are your scars, Whit? I want to see them." He runs his nose along my own. "All of them."

I don't even think before I respond, don't filter my response to the bland, rehearsed one I normally would. "When someone who's supposed to love you treats you as if you're disposable, it's difficult not to see your value as less than nothing."

Cole squeezes his eyes together like I've caused him physical pain. When he opens them, he pulls back just enough to pin me with his stare. "You are so much more than nothing, sweetheart. You're the opposite. You're everything."

He leans in and kisses my forehead, his hand at the back of my head.

"It's okay to lean on someone," he mumbles against my skin before pulling back to look at me. "Sometimes. When it's the right person." He brushes his thumb over my bottom lip, stares at me for another second.

"Excuse me . . . could one of you take a picture of us with the view of the city behind us?"

Both of us separate quickly with wide eyes as if we've just been caught doing something we shouldn't have. And I suppose that's true.

I turn to see a middle-aged couple beside us holding out a camera toward us.

"Uh, sure." Cole gets up off the ledge and follows them a little farther down the railing, where they strike a pose for the camera. He takes a few shots, directing them a little to make sure they get the best picture, and then returns the camera to them. They thank him before heading on their way.

Without mentioning the kiss, he returns and takes his seat beside me, picks up his sandwich and continues eating his lunch like nothing of consequence just happened. And maybe it didn't for him.

But my entire world just shifted beneath me the same as if another catastrophic earthquake struck the city.

We both gaze out over the city while we finish eating. The fog rolls in off the Pacific Ocean, swallowing the Golden Gate

Bridge until just the red steel tips are visible. I feel a lot like that bridge—everything I see, feel, and touch seems to be Cole. I'm surrounded by him, overcome and overwhelmed every time I'm around him, and I'm left gasping for air, barely surviving the deluge that is this man's power over me.

*chapter*

# SIXTEEN

*I* SIT IN THE booth at the pub—not the Thirsty Monk, but a different one around the corner from my grandparents' house—waiting for Lennon to show.

She's late. No surprise there.

I asked her to meet me here because Tahlia is still out of town dealing with a business crisis and I need to talk to her about what's going on with Cole. Or isn't. I don't know what to think given how he acted after that kiss at Twin Peaks. Lennon has more experience with the opposite sex than Tahl and I combined, so she's a good person to mine for knowledge. Hell, she might have more experience than a Playboy bunny, now that I think about it.

She's ten minutes late already so I decide to do something productive while waiting for her. I pull out my phone to look up the latest job listings. Maybe something new has been posted that I can apply to. Yes, I still want my dream job at the news station, but I haven't heard anything from them yet and I can't afford to sit around with all my eggs in that basket.

The bartender comes over and I order myself a rum and

seven, steering way clear of any whiskey because this guy is cute, though nowhere near as hot as Cole. Still, I don't need any more bartender problems than I already have.

I check another job site, but there's nothing suited to my talents that I haven't already applied for. I sigh and shove my phone back into my purse, just about to pull my journal out of my bag to record some of my thoughts, when Lennon arrives.

In she comes, sauntering over to the booth like she's not at all running late. Her coat is in her hand and she's in a pair of skinny jeans with stylish rips down the front and a clingy t-shirt that reads 'Fries Before Guys'.

"Hey, bitch," she says with a smile and slides in across from me.

"Hello, whore."

This is something we do from time to time and we both know it's meant in jest, neither of us taking offense.

"I wish," she says. "This week has been a real dry spell." She tosses her purse beside her on the bench seat.

"What happened to that guy you were with when I called from Cole's house that morning?"

She waves me off and rolls her eyes. "He got clingy."

Ah. There's nothing that Lennon hates more than a guy who expects something more from her than just her vagina. As soon as he shows the tiniest glimpse of wanting to move the relationship into more serious territory, she has him half out of her bed.

"Can I get you something to drink?" The cute bartender is back and places my drink in front of me.

Lennon is immediately sizing him up, not at all hiding the fact that she's checking him out and liking what she sees. She smiles and bats her eyelashes at him, turning on the charm. "What would you recommend?"

He gives her a half-crooked smile, having gotten her memo.

"I make a killer Mountain Dew Me."

"I bet you do." She bites her bottom lip and I roll my eyes, but neither of them are paying any attention to me. "I tend to prefer my *cock*tails," she says, emphasizing the word 'cock,' "a little rougher than that."

Somehow, she says this with a straight face.

"Give me a minute and I'll bring you back something to wet your whistle."

Lennon's grin grows. "How about I wet your whistle later?"

"Okay, enough," I interrupt. "We need to talk." I shift my attention to the guy. "Can you just bring her a drink?"

He shoots me a half-annoyed look before he leaves the table.

"Why did you do that?" Lennon whines after he's left.

"Really? You two were eye-fucking each other and I'm sitting right here in crisis mode. After we're done, feel free to screw him six ways to Sunday."

"Oh, sweetie," she says and pats my hand like I'm a child. "I'll screw him six ways before the sun comes up tomorrow."

I let out an exasperated sigh.

She laughs. "Now, what's going on with Cole?"

"How do you know it has to do with him?" I reach for my drink and take a sip.

This time it's Lennon rolling her eyes. "Please. I know you."

"What does that mean?"

"It means that any time you can't control something . . . like your feelings for a guy . . . you freak out. You don't like relying on someone and when you're falling for a guy you have to give up some of your control and independence. You don't like that." She shrugs as if it's obvious.

I sit silent for a moment, processing what she's just said. All I can come up with is that she's right. I don't want to rely on anyone else. I've been let down too many times. It's better just to count on yourself. That way, no one has the power to hurt you.

"You know I'm right," she says in a sing-song voice.

The bartender reappears and sets a large, red drink down in front of her.

"Here you go. I made a Suck, Bang and Blow special for you," he says with a wink.

Lennon leans forward as seductively as possible and with no hands wraps her lips around the straw and takes a sip. "Mmm," she moans with way too much enthusiasm.

"You like?" he asks.

She flicks her gaze to his crotch before responding. "I do."

"That's some pretty nice ink you have there." He points to her arm, sporting a full sleeve of tattoos. "I've been thinking of adding to my own. Where'd you get it done?"

"At my own shop," she says proudly. Lennon reaches for her purse and pulls out a business card adorned with her 'What Are You Inking?' logo and information, then passes it to him.

"Cool," he says.

"Take that for now," she says. "I'll come talk to you about it after we're done. You can show me where you're thinking of putting it and maybe then I'll show you my version of Suck, Bang and Blow."

He smiles like he's just won the damn lottery. "Abso-fuck-ing-lutely." He grins at her for another second before heading back over to the bar.

Lennon immediately turns her attention back to me. "Okay, spill. What's happening with you and Cole?" She pivots so easily away from her last conversation that it's like she didn't just offer herself up to some guy in front of me.

And so, I tell her about our agreement to get along and work together for Tahlia and Chase's sake and about our time checking out all the places and then finally the kiss.

"So, what do I do?" I ask when I'm done.

"Hmm." That's all she says after I pour my heart out.

"What does that mean?"

She puts her finger up. "Hang on. I'm processing."

I take another long sip of my drink while I wait. And wait. "Well?"

"I think it's a question of whether you think there is really something between you or if you're just attracted to him and want to bump uglies with him. You do want to bang him again, right?"

"Well, he tells me I referred to his junk as unicorn cock the night we hooked up, so it's safe to say I was into it."

"Unicorn cock!" Lennon practically shouts and smacks her hand down on the table in front of her. "That's awesome. Why didn't I think of that? I need to get that on a t-shirt."

"Can you be serious for a second?"

"Sorry." She works to compose herself then asks. "Well, which is it? Are there feelings between you two or do you just want him balls deep in your business?"

"How are we even friends?" I shake my head.

She winks. "You love me."

"Sadly, yes. And to answer your question I don't really know. After everything that happened all those years ago . . . I don't know if I could ever really let that go. I mean, maybe he's matured since then, I'd like to think that I have also, but still. He's responsible for so much going wrong in my life—"

"Does he know that?"

"Are you kidding me?" I screw my face up and look over at her and then pick up my drink.

"So, hit it and quit it. Get it out of your system." She shrugs like it's just that easy. "But if this is going to be *something*, Whit, you have to tell him about that night. All of it."

I decide to ignore her last comment. "How do you do it? How do you find it so easy to walk away from them all?"

She gives a small laugh. "It's different. I can love 'em and leave 'em because I don't care about them. I'm there for the adventure and the good times. You . . . you care. Even though you don't want to." She gives me a sad smile and reaches across the table to squeeze my hand.

Damn it. She's right.

"What about Tahlia?" I ask. "I don't like keeping this from her, but she's got so much going on right now."

"Tell me about it. Every time I talk to her lately I think she's one second away from a complete mental breakdown. I thought weddings were supposed to be fun?"

"Should I tell her?"

Lennon shakes her head. "No. Not unless you think it's going somewhere. If you're just screwing around, then have your fun and mention it *after* the wedding's over and you've both moved on."

My gut is telling me the same thing . . . that one more piece of straw on the camel's back would break Tahl. She has enough going on right now and doesn't need to be bothered with my problems.

"I think you're right. Thanks babe."

She picks up her drink and clinks it with mine. "Anytime. This bitch has got your back."

"I'm the bitch. You're the whore, remember?"

She laughs. "True enough. And in that vein, if we're done here, I'm about to go shore up my prospects over there." She nods toward the bar and the bartender who's still watching her every move.

"Go." I laugh and wave her off.

I need to adopt a little of Lennon's personality. If I'm going to have to be around Cole again I'm either going to have to take it as the fun it has the potential to be or ignore my desire completely. That feels like a tall order, but I'm not one to back down from a challenge.

As soon as the thought crosses my mind, my phone rings and presents me with my next challenge. But this is a good one.

# chapter
# SEVENTEEN

N ERVES HAVE ME SHAKING like a Stepford wife being weaned off Valium. I open the heavy glass doors of the skyscraper downtown and step into the WHFI lobby. When she called the other night to offer me an on-camera test, the human resources lady said to go to the thirty-first floor this time.

I suck in a deep breath to pull myself together as my heels click on the tile floor while I cross the large lobby toward the elevators. I chose to wear a navy pencil skirt with cream-coloured cami underneath the matching jacket. It's uncomfortable as hell, but it's the closest thing I have to something that screams newscaster.

Right before I enter the elevator my phone vibrates in my purse. I pull it out to take a look as the elevator starts and stops, letting people on and off.

*Cole: Tahlia mentioned that you got a call back. Good luck today. Head over to the bar after and I'll buy you a celebratory drink. No whiskey I promise. ;)*

Wow. That's almost sweet of him, though I'm not sure

what to think given the fact that we haven't even spoken since the kiss. Even so, I smile down at my phone, probably looking like a lunatic. The elevator dings again and when I glance up I realize it's at my floor.

"Excuse me. Excuse me." I push my way to the front of the car and make it out right before the doors pancake me. I take another quick glance at my phone before I put it back into my purse.

"I see that guy's still putting a smile on your face."

My head snaps up to see Kelsey standing in front of me. I'm impressed that I even remember her name because I usually have the memory of a goldfish for things like that.

"You got a call back, too," I say, ignoring her comment about Cole.

She nods enthusiastically and I take in her outfit. Kelsey has on a pair of black cigarette pants and a dressy, patterned tank top. She looks like she's ready for a night out with the girls and I look like I'm ready for church.

"Okay, why do I look like Dorothy from *The Golden Girls* compared to you?"

She laughs. "You're so funny."

She's cute. She thinks I'm joking.

"Really though. The least I could have done was go for the slutty one, Blanche."

"When HR called, she said to wear something I'd typically wear if I was headed out to dinner."

Crap. I must have missed the memo.

"She didn't tell me that." My stomach feels like I have a carnival ride spinning around and around inside it and I suck in a breath and place a hand over my middle.

"We're interviewing for different jobs. Maybe it's just the sportscaster position they wanted in more casual clothes. She said they're trying to appeal to a younger demographic."

"Yeah, maybe." I chew on my bottom lip for a second. "How did you do?"

Now she looks nervous. "I think I did okay." She shrugs. "It's hard to say. They don't really comment or anything after you're done."

"Okay, well, I'd better get in there."

"Good luck," she says brightly.

"Thanks. Same to you."

As I head off to my on-camera testing I find myself hoping that she gets the position just as much as myself.

THE STUDIO LIGHTS BLARING down on me feel oppressive, like a heavy blanket smothering me, but I smile into the camera.

"Okay, so just read from the teleprompter and deliver the lines while looking straight into the camera," the producer says, standing back by the cameraman. "We'll cut to tape and when that's finished rolling you're up again. Don't worry about the content at this point. We just want to see how you do on camera."

I suck in a big breath and nod.

"Do you have any questions before we begin?"

"No, I think I'm good."

"Okay then. Roll tape." He counts me down and I smile while I wait for the theme music for the station before I begin.

The words scroll past on the teleprompter and I speak in my most natural, articulated voice without giving too much thought to the content.

"Last night was a big one for the San Francisco Film Society as they hosted yet another successful opening night for the city's annual Film Fest. Producers, actors, and screenwriters alike joined the public for the debut of some of this year's most talked-about films. While everyone had plenty to say about what they saw on the big screen, the fans' eyes outside were on some of the up-and-coming stars who stepped out onto the red carpet."

The prompter says, "Cut to tape," and so I smile in what I hope is a natural way at the camera.

The tape starts and I look behind me to where something has caught my eye. The TV built into the wall replays footage of expensively dressed people smiling and posing for photos on a red carpet, some of whom I recognize as being actors and actress who've recently broken onto the scene. It cuts to an interview with a blonde woman I don't recognize and then they pan to the man she's with.

A man I know.

Because he had his tongue down my throat a few days ago.

Cole is there with his arm wrapped around the waist of an exotic-looking woman. I know for sure it's him because his name is listed underneath as if the universe is really trying to rub it in.

My mouth dries and my throat tightens in response.

I don't think it's recent because the Cole on screen looks a little different than he does now, but seeing him on there enjoying the company of another woman stings. It's a reminder of who he is and how he treated me all those years ago. And then I think of what was taken away from me back then and my heart begins to beat harder in my chest as the memories of the disappointment and hurt I dealt with flood through me, filling up every crevice.

I stare on as the interviewer finishes up with her questions for Cole and then the screen goes blank.

*I will not think about this now. I will not think about this now.*

Somehow, I manage to turn and direct my attention back to the teleprompter and carry on with a smile. Once I'm done, the producer thanks me for coming in and telling me that I should hear something within the next week or two.

Nothing seems to be going according to plan lately and I leave there with my fingers and toes crossed that this might be the one thing that works out the way I'm hoping. I've had enough surprises lately.

*I* DECIDE THAT I *will* head over to the Thirsty Monk to see if Cole is around. Besides, we still have a couple of locations to visit and we need to discuss when we're going to do that anyway. These are the kinds of excuses you tell yourself when you're trying to justify your behavior. I just don't want to face the fact that I shouldn't accept Cole's invitation to hang out.

Opting for the bus over Uber seems like the responsible thing to do since I need to watch my spending, so it takes me a while to make it to the bar. By the time I do the heels I'm wearing are stabbing my feet and I just want to sit down.

As soon as I enter the pub I glance around. There's only a few other people here, which I suppose is normal since it's just after lunch on a week day. I spot Cole speaking to the blonde bartender from the night I met him. They appear to be deep in conversation and I don't want to interrupt so I slink off and sit in a booth in the back corner. I can still see them from here and I watch as Cole's face turns serious and he places a hand on the girl's cheek. He nods and then she says something else. She's gazing up into his eyes like he's her savior or something but damn it, I can't see Cole's expression. They embrace and a sickly feeling invades my stomach, which I know is not good news because I should not be feeling anything other than disinterest at the fact that Cole is hugging another woman. But that combined with the tape I saw at the audition has me wondering why I even headed over here.

They separate and she goes back behind the bar to do whatever it is stupid girls who hug their bosses do, and Cole turns to head in the direction of the kitchen. He must spot me out of the corner of his eye because he whirls back and locks his gaze with mine from across the room.

There's a brief second where his eyes flare and a panicked look creeps into them, but it's gone just as fast. I wonder if he's concerned about what I saw. The earlier expression is replaced with a slow, easy smile as his long strides eat up the distance between us.

He looks good today. Damn good. He's wearing a worn pair of jeans and a plaid lumbersexual shirt that's fitted enough to see how fit he is underneath. His sandy brown hair is a little messy and though he's not sporting a beard, the five o'clock shadow is in full effect.

"Hey." He slides into the booth on the opposite side of me. Cole smiles and it seems genuine, which is good because I was beginning to think that I was a complete idiot to come here. "How did the interview go?"

"It went okay. I managed not to make a complete ass of myself, so that's a bonus." I shrug, feigning nonchalance I don't really feel.

"Any idea when you'll know?"

"They said they'd call."

"Well, at least they didn't say thanks but no thanks." I think he's trying to give me confidence about the whole thing, but there's only one thing on my mind.

"It was interesting actually. I had to read off the teleprompter and then they cut to tape and there you were. Being interviewed by one of the reporters on screen."

He leans back into the booth and laughs a little. "Really? What the hell was I talking about?"

"It was the film festival here in town. You and your date were being interviewed."

He looks amused. "Oh, I remember that." He laughs and shakes his head. At some memory, I guess. "A friend introduced me to Sarah Morgan before she hit the big time and I agreed to go with her."

"Sounds fun," I say, sounding less than enthused.

"Do you know her? She's a crazy bitch. I couldn't get out of there fast enough that night."

"Oh. I thought maybe you two had been a thing."

He shakes his head, his eyebrows almost raising to his hairline. "Not likely. I like my women low-drama and she's about as far away from that as you can get."

I simply nod. I'm sure I've probably played my cards and made it obvious that the idea bothers me, but if Cole picks up on it he gives me a free pass because he doesn't say anything about it.

Underneath the table I toe off one of my high heels and then the other because the leather digging into my skin is beginning to feel like either a new form of BDSM or prisoner-of-war torture.

One of my shoes drops noisily to the floor below and Cole leans back to look under the table.

"Sorry. I can't wear these any longer. They're killing me."

He chuckles. "I don't understand how you women wear those things. I mean, I'm grateful, but your feet must sting like a bitch in them."

"Just a little." I grimace. I bend one of my legs so that I can reach my foot and begin massaging a sore spot.

"Here, let me." Cole gestures for me to stretch my legs

across to the other side of the booth. I'm not sure what to think. But since my feet are screaming for some relief I don't think long about it. I lean against the bench seat and stretch my legs across and into Cole's lap. His hands delve beneath the table and take one of my feet gently into his palms.

He begins massaging my foot and oh, my God, I think I could orgasm right here in this booth, it feels so good.

I let a small, satisfied moan escape and close my eyes for a moment.

Cole chuckles. "The look on your face right now reminds me of when you come."

My eyes snap open. "Excuse me?"

His thumb presses into a divine spot in my arch and my eyes drift closed for a second. He lets a low chuckle escape again.

"I said the expression on your face when you moaned reminded me of when you come."

It's safe to say that listening to Cole talk about me coming is a turn-on based on the way my nipples stiffen and I grow wet between the legs.

"H-how would you know?"

That lopsided smirk he has, the one that could probably talk me into doing almost anything with him—and for all I know did that one night we were together—forms on his face and he just grins at me without answering.

"You're making that up." I huff and cross my arms over my chest.

He simply shrugs. "Okay." He sets down the foot he's working on and exchanges it for the other one, gently removing my other shoe.

"Okay?" I say with as much attitude as I can jam into those four little words.

"Okay, if you say so." He presses his fingers deep into the balls of my foot and damn it, my eyes close again.

He chuckles.

"Seriously, Cole. Tell me."

"Uh-uh-uh. You'd better be nice to me or I don't have to tell you anything. Remember our deal?"

"That reminds me. You didn't tell me anything the last time we were together and I was nice to you all day. You owe me."

"Hmm. That's right, but you're not being nice right now so I think that negates any previous interactions."

I clench my teeth and suck the skin from my cheeks between them just so I have something to bite down on. In my best sing-song voice I continue. "Cole, will you please tell me what you're talking about and whether you're making that up?" I give him a saccharine smile.

"I suppose that will do."

And then he doesn't say anything.

"Well?"

"You are so easy to rile up, you know that?" He chuckles.

I release another huff of frustration. "Would. You. Please. Just. Tell. Me?" I grit out.

"All right. All right." He locks stares with me and doesn't as much as blink when he says, "You came on my hand."

"I did not." I don't know why I'm arguing because it's not like I actually *know* what happened most of that night.

"You did." He has a smug smile on his face. "Would you like me to tell you about it?"

Pride makes me want to pretend that I don't care what he has to say, but curiosity and the need to know exactly what we did together win out. "Please," I say in a small voice.

He leans over the table a bit and lowers his voice to speak. "Well, after we got back to my place and you were all over me you told me how turned on you were and how wet I made you." Heat rushes into my cheeks and I stiffen and try to pull my feet away from him.

His forehead creases for a second and he pulls them back into his lap and then switches feet again.

"Then I told you that I wanted proof and so first I took your shoes off. Then I slowly peeled your pants down your legs and you stepped out of them. You stood there in your lace underwear looking like every man's wet dream come to life and I couldn't resist. I pushed my hand past the waistband of your underwear, over your mound and between the swollen lips of your pussy. You were soaked and it was such a fucking turn-on that I'm surprised I didn't come in my pants right then and there. I finger-fucked you until you came on my hand. I haven't been able to get the expression on your face out of my head since it happened. So much so that I've jacked off to that image in my mind almost every day."

He shifts in his seat and . . . is that? It is.

He's hard as a rock underneath my feet and I know he knows that I know.

*Way to make it sound like a* Friends *episode, Whit.*

His gaze locks with mine and he stops massaging my feet for a second. We sit there like two statues for a moment and I can't resist. I gently push my foot down to get a better feel for what lies beneath the denim. His long, hard erection under my foot leaves me wanting more. I shift my foot up and down the length of him and his eyes drift closed while he sucks in a breath.

He opens his eyes and pins me with a stare, his eyes full of lust and promises. Promises I really want him to follow through on.

"Can I get you something to drink?"

The voice beside me startles me and I just about jump from my seat. I move to pull my legs away from Cole's lap, but he grabs a hold of my ankle and stops me.

"Do you want anything?" Cole asks, probably because I'm still sitting here like a mute. He seems like he's trying to hold back a laugh, but nothing about this situation is funny.

I realize that his waist is under the table so the bartender can't see, but still. I'm not Cole's girlfriend, I'm not his anything and the idea of someone else knowing what's going on is mortifying.

"I'm probably not staying, so I'm good, thanks."

She glances between the two of us several times before she gives us each a small smile and backs away. She's not exactly bitchy to me, but she's not all that friendly either.

"I should probably go." I pull my feet away from Cole and this time he lets me.

"No, wait." He places his hand over the top of where mine rests on the table. "Why are you rushing off?" For some reason, he seems genuinely perplexed by this, though I can't imagine why.

"This"—I motion with my free hand between the two of us—"cannot happen. What just happened was out of hand."

He tilts his head to the side and grins. "Don't you mean, out of foot?"

I roll my eyes and scoot to the edge of the booth. "I'm serious. I shouldn't have done that."

Cole shrugs. "No complaints here."

"And that kiss the other day. That can't happen again either. Anything between us isn't going to go anywhere, so there's—"

"And why is that again?"

I can't say what I'm thinking, which is that I don't think I'll ever be able to get past the underlying resentment I feel for the man who's been pivotal in my life veering off course. Though that resentment seems to be taking a back seat lately.

"Because you're you. And I'm me." Cole is a ladies' man and I've been disappointed enough by the men in my life to know to stay well clear of a guy like him.

He removes his hand from over the top of mine as if my skin is on fire. "Right. Whatever the hell that means."

"Can we just concentrate on what we have to do for Tahlia and Chase and forget all that ever happened?"

"Do you want to forget what happened that night with us, too?"

"First I need to *know* what happened so that I can try to forget. And you're not being very helpful in that regard."

"We have a deal."

"That's right we do. Part of that deal was that we'd keep our hands off each other and—"

"True, but we never said anything about feet."

"I'm serious, Cole."

He raises his hands up in a placating gesture. "Okay. Tell me what it is you want from me."

Such a loaded question and he knows it, based on the grin on his face.

I cross my arms over my chest and cock a hip. Cole's gaze darts down to my cleavage and I immediately uncross my arms. "I want you to pick me up tomorrow at eleven so that we can go check out the last few of the locations. Can you do that?"

"Consider it done," he says and does an exaggerated bow.

"Stop bowing. I'm not royalty."

He scoffs and shakes his head before running a hand through his hair. "To the right guy, you are." Without another word, he pivots on his heel and heads deeper into the pub, leaving me stunned and speechless.

*chapter*

# NINETEEN

*J*'M CUDDLED ON A chair in the living room writing in my journal. Sparky glares at me from the floor, yelping every so often. Eventually, I can't stand it.

"Fine, come up here, you little monkey." I place my notebook down open face on the side table and lean forward. I pick up the little fur ball, placing him in my lap. In return he uses my chest as a prop for his front paws and licks my cheek in thanks.

"Ew, Sparky. Gross." I use my shirt sleeve to wipe his doggie saliva off my cheek. He doesn't seem to get the hint because he just stands there panting happily. I pick him up and turn him around, placing him across my lap. When I scratch behind his ears he tilts his head back and closes his eyes.

I roll mine in response, realizing that I'm slowly becoming the slave to this master. When I stop and pick up my book again he lets out a little whine and lowers his head to rest on my leg. I can't help but think how cute he looks. Then I remind myself of that pair of shoes of mine that he ate last week.

A little while later my grandparents join me. I look up to see my grandpa shuffle into the room. I've noticed that he holds onto the furniture sometimes as he navigates his way through the house, almost as if he uses it for balance. I've questioned them both on it, but they insist it's nothing—just all part of getting older.

"I see you two are becoming fast friends," my grandma says.

I glance down at Sparky for a second. "He kind of forces you to. He won't quit until you give him what he wants."

"Reminds me of someone else I know," my grandpa says before taking a seat in one of the chairs.

My grandma sits and looks over at him. "She was a stubborn child, wasn't she?"

They both laugh and I can tell that they're both remembering something from when I was younger.

"I wasn't *that* bad."

My grandma tilts her head. "Sweetheart, you've always known what you want and haven't been afraid to go after it."

There's not much I can argue against there so I shrug. When both of your birth parents abandon you, you learn quickly that the only person you can ever truly rely on is yourself.

"I'm going to grab a drink. Anyone else want anything?" I ask.

"Can you grab Sparky a treat? I usually give him one a little before lunch," my grandma says.

"Sure thing. Where are they?" I ask and set aside my journal.

"In the drawer beside the cutlery."

"Okay." I lift Sparky up and rise from the chair.

"If you keep pampering that dog so much, Edna, he's never going to want to leave," my grandpa says.

I laugh as I make my way into the kitchen and then yank open the drawer we affectionately always referred to as the junk drawer when I was growing up. Since I don't see the treats immediately I rifle through and end up pulling out a few notepads, some Scotch tape, and various pens. An envelope catches my eye and I pull it out. There's a Hillside Retirement Residence logo on the corner.

I know I shouldn't snoop, but I'm curious and I know that if I ask my grandparents what this is about I won't get a straight answer. So instead of doing the right thing and respecting my grandparents' privacy, I pull the papers out to examine them.

It's an application for the retirement residence and my grandmother has filled it out. The bottom required her to sign and date it and I realize that she filled this out the day before I called and asked if it would be okay for me to move back in with them for a while.

Guilt, hot and fast, pours into my veins, heating me from the inside out. Neither my grandma nor my grandpa has mentioned moving to a retirement community to me. But of course they didn't. They've always put me first regardless of how it would inconvenience their own lives. Case in point—raising a child they never should have had to be responsible for.

I debate whether I should mention anything to them, but quickly decide against it. They'll only put me off and say it's not a big deal, they're happy to have me, blah, blah. But in reality, I've prevented them from moving on to the next phase of their life because I haven't been able to move on to the next phase of my own life.

Nails click on the floor and I look behind me to see Sparky strut into the kitchen. He must sense something is amiss because he walks over to me and nudges my leg with his head and sits down beside it.

"Are you having trouble finding them?" my grandma calls out from the living room.

"Just found them!" I try to keep my voice light and easy, all things I'm not feeling as I shove the papers back into the envelope. I move a couple other things around and finally spot a small bag of treats and pull one out.

Sparky trails me by only a few inches as I walk back to the living room.

"Here you go." I hand the treat out to my grandma.

"Oh, you can give it to him, sweetheart. You seem to be his favorite anyway."

Melancholy invades my chest. My grandma is always so sweet and she never fails to put me first. I need to do right by them both and find a job so that I can stand on my own two feet again and allow them to live their golden years the way they want. They're the only two people I've ever allowed myself to rely on in my life and it's time for me to prove that I really do only need myself.

Me getting that job at the news is even more important now, but if that doesn't happen I'm going to have to take the first thing I can find. I owe it to the two of them and to myself.

"**Y**OU DON'T SEEM LIKE your usual self. Everything okay?" Cole asks from the driver's seat of his Jeep.

We're headed to our second destination of the day. The first venue was a total bust. The pictures online that Tahlia sent me made it look special enough, so I understand why she chose it, but it was worn, dated, and in need of updating. In no way was it fit for the union of the two most prominent families in the city.

"Just a lot on my mind, that's all." I continue to stare out at the gray autumn day.

"I'm here if you need to vent."

I glance over and ours eyes lock for a second before safety dictates he look back at the street in front of us. "I'm sure you have better things to do than listen to me complain."

He reaches over and squeezes my leg, just over the top of my knee. It's not a sexual thing at all, but any time Cole touches me I can't help but wonder what it would be like to let him explore my body further.

"I don't know if you noticed, but all I have is time right

now." He motions to the line of traffic out the front window. "We're both running around for a wedding that isn't ours and we're trapped. Vent away."

A small, sad smile forms on my face. "I found out that my grandparents planned to move to a retirement community right before I returned home."

"Okay . . ." He shifts a bit in his seat. "Why does that upset you?"

I let my head fall back against the headrest and stare up at the roof. "Before I returned home I was working at the local paper in Sacramento. I'd been there since I finished college, but I was fired, laid off . . . it's complicated. Anyway, I tried to find another job in town, but it was a bust. When my finances ran out I had to move back in with my grandparents here in the city."

"Why does it sound like there's something more to you losing your job than just an ordinary downsizing?" he asks.

This is going to go from a venting session to a full-blown therapy session if I'm not careful. "I made the colossal mistake of sleeping with my boss." I cover my face in shame.

The oppressive weight of silence in the car threatens to suffocate me. I can't bring myself to look over at Cole.

"And?"

I sense no judgment in his voice and so I let my hands fall to my lap and peek over at him. "We fooled around for a while and I thought we were dating, but apparently he was dating a few people. Basically, his new treat of the week was uncomfortable with me being around and so he let me go." My description, as distasteful as it sounds, is being generous as to the character of my former boss. But Cole doesn't need to hear all the dirty details.

Cole presses on the brake and the car comes to a complete stop. A moment later his large hand covers mine and squeezes.

"Whitney, forgive me for saying this, but your boss sounds like a class-A asshole. It's his loss."

"It was stupid of me to start anything with him in the first place. I'd heard rumors about what he was like."

Cole shrugs. "Maybe, but it doesn't make the way he treated you okay. You deserve to be treated like the prize that you really are."

I hold his gaze and the attraction between us intensifies until we're both leaning in toward one another. We both move slowly, and I wonder if he wants to remember this moment as much as me. My lips tingle when we're only an inch apart and my eyes drift shut. I feel his breath inching closer and my heart races, waiting for the touch of his lips to mine.

The loud ring of a phone echoes throughout the vehicle.

My eyes fly open and we both jump apart with wide eyes. I half expect to see my grandpa's face in the window like when he caught me kissing Bobby Sinclair in his beat-up Honda my sophomore year.

The ringing pierces the silence again, dragging me out of my thoughts. Cole must have his phone connected to his Bluetooth in the car. He pushes a button and the ringing stops.

"Yeah?" he answers.

"Hey, man. I think we might have an issue with one of the batches. Any chance you can swing by to check it out?" a man on the other end of the line says.

Cole glances over at me and I don't miss the way he tightens his grip on the steering wheel. "Sure thing. Be there in fifteen." He pushes another button and hangs up. "Mind if we make a quick stop before we go to the next place?"

"It's not like I have anywhere to be." I shrug.

"Thanks."

He doesn't offer any further info so I don't ask, figuring I'll see where we're headed once we get there. His mood has done a one-eighty from minutes before when we almost played tonsil hockey and I have no idea why, but I have a feeling I'm about to get a better glimpse at who this man really is. And I'm not sure he's happy about that.

⁓

A SHORT TIME LATER we pull into a commercial area in the outskirts of the city and park in front of a medium-size industrial building.

"I don't think this should take very long. Do you want to wait in the car?"

*Hell, no, I don't want to wait in the car. I'm way too curious for that.*

"Mind if I join you?"

He seems resigned when he replies. "Okay."

"So what is this place?" I ask as we walk along a concrete path to the glass doors in the front of the building.

"This is Rock Hard Whiskey. I own this place."

"Wait." I tug on his arm and pull him to a stop. "You own a whiskey distillery?"

"Yep."

"How come you never mentioned it?"

"It never came up." He turns and continues to the entrance.

I follow him into a small reception area. It's somewhat dated and appears to have whatever furniture was there when the building was originally built. A woman with long, dark hair sits behind the lone desk working away on a computer.

She glances up when she hears the door open and smiles at Cole as we enter. "Hey, boss man. Did Brady call you?"

"Yep. He out back?"

She smiles and nods.

"Ashley, this is Whitney." Cole gestures between the two us.

"Nice to meet you, Whitney."

"Same here," I say. Ashley is an attractive woman, probably

in her late thirties if I had to guess. She seems genuinely fond of Cole, but not in the same way the bartender who works for him at the Thirsty Monk does.

"Do you want to stay here while I sort this out?" Cole asks me. "If you want I can take you on a tour of the place after I sort out this problem. It's not much, but—"

"I'd love that." And I mean it. I've never seen a distillery in my life. Actually, I have no idea how you even make whiskey so I'm looking forward to finding out.

I take a seat in one of the three chairs in the small foyer. I have a feeling it's coming, though it takes Ashley longer than I expect to ask. It's a full twenty seconds before she strikes.

"So, what's going on with you and Cole?" she whispers conspiratorially.

I smile. "We're just friends. His brother is marrying my friend and we're both in the wedding party. We're helping them out with the planning."

She turns her head to the side and screws up her lips a bit before speaking again. "But you like him."

"Excuse me?" I try hard not to let the shock of what she just said show on my face.

"You can tell me. I won't say anything to him about it."

I have a feeling that's about as far from the truth as you can get. "Like I said. We're just friends." I smile again, hoping she'll drop it. There's nothing bitchy or aggressive about her interrogation. She comes across more like she's genuinely curious and maybe wants the inside scoop more than anything.

"Damn. I wish he'd find himself a nice girl." She sighs and rests her chin on her hand. "You look like a *nice* girl."

"Thanks?" She's quiet for a moment and I decide to change the subject while I have the chance. "So how long has he had this distillery?"

"A little more than three years. I've been here since day

one." Ashley sits up a little straighter and puffs her chest out a bit, obviously proud of that fact.

"Is the business doing well?" As soon as the question is out of my mouth I realize what a gold-digger I sound like. "What I mean is, how are things going?"

My remark doesn't faze Ashley. "Pretty well. We've kept our heads above water the past couple years and we're finally starting to make some headway. Right now, we're only on the West Coast and mostly just in California. Cole is working on getting a meeting with a big distributor. If he nails it, we'll have distribution nationwide."

"Wow. That's exciting!"

"It really is," she says and then frowns.

"Everything okay?"

She waves me off. "Oh, I'm just a worrier, that's all. It's the mom in me."

"What's there to worry about?" I set my purse on the chair beside me. "It sounds like everything is going well."

She glances to the hallway Cole disappeared to moments ago and turns back my way. "It is. I just . . . I know Cole would like to spend more time here and I fear that he's going to have to make a decision that won't be easy for him."

"Between this and his father's company?" I ask, figuring it out on my own.

Ashley nods.

"I'm sure if he tried to make a go at this and it didn't work out his father would welcome him back with open arms, no?"

She shrugs. "It's complicated."

Interesting. It seems like maybe I'm not the only one with daddy issues. I wonder if that's why Cole reacted so strongly when I divulged the information about my parents, or lack thereof.

Ashley and I chat for another ten minutes about our mutual

love for classic movies, baseball, and Ryan Reynolds.

Cole finally returns, looking a lot more relaxed than he did when we arrived. "Sorry that took so long. You ready for the grand tour?"

"Absolutely." I reach for my purse and stand from the chair, directing my attention to Ashley. "Thanks for chatting with me while I waited."

"The pleasure was all mine." She turns her attention to Cole. "You'd be a fool to let this one get away, Cole. Better man up before someone else makes a move."

Maybe I don't like Ashley as much as I thought.

My face heats and I can't make eye contact with Cole so I turn and walk back out to his Jeep, pulling my coat tighter around myself. He jogs up from behind me.

"You don't want the grand tour anymore?"

I don't turn around when I answer. "We should probably get moving so we have time to hit all the places before they close."

"Sorry about Ashley," he calls out from behind me. "She can be a little much some times."

I come to a stop beside his Jeep and wonder whether he's sorry because he thinks she embarrassed me or if he's sorry because the idea is so preposterous to him.

I decide not to ask. There are some questions you're better off not knowing the answer to.

*chapter*

# TWENTY-ONE

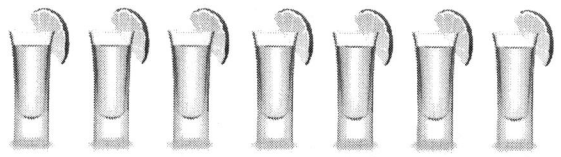

F INALLY, NEAR THE END of a long day, we're headed to our final stop. So far nothing has beat the Reserve that we saw the other day and since we've both been dragging ass we decide to make a quick pit stop at Starbucks to refuel.

Turns out Cole is a Grande Americano kinda guy.

All afternoon I've been wanting to turn the topic of conversation back to his whiskey business, but I'm too chickenshit. Since our day is coming to a close soon I feel like it's now or never and so I finally gather up the courage to ask what's been bothering me. "Why didn't you mention your whiskey business before?" It's not like he owes me an explanation, but it just seems like something that would have come up before now, given all the time we've spent together lately.

Cole sighs and glances away from traffic, over at me for a second. "Are you usually eager to share your failures with someone?"

My forehead creases. "How is it a failure? It looked like a pretty legitimate business to me."

He lifts his Starbucks cup from the holder and takes a large sip before answering. "Maybe it's not a complete failure. But some months I'm barely in the black. Something my father never fails to remind me of." Bitterness creeps into his voice.

"He doesn't approve?"

I can only see his profile—regardless, it's clear that he has a frown on his face. "No, my father doesn't approve of anything that doesn't involve increasing the Webber family fortune. Why do you think he and Chase get along so well? They're exactly alike in that sense."

"I didn't realize that you don't get along with your father that well." I shift in my seat to face him better.

Cole shrugs. "My entire life has been spent trying to prove myself to my father. To him my distillery is a cute little side project that I'm dabbling in." Sadness and disappointment ring clear in his voice and I want to reach out and hug him or something. Anything to make him feel better.

"But it's not to you . . ."

He shakes his head. "No. I'm passionate about it. It's what I want to build into a big business some day." He laughs a bit and there's a nervous edge to it as if he's said too much.

"I'm sure that will happen." I can't help myself. I reach out and squeeze the hand closest to me before I think better of it. It's not until he turns his hand over and squeezes mine back that I pull away.

"I think I can get an appointment with a distributor I've been talking to. If I can convince him to take Rock Hard Whiskey on, I won't have to worry about breaking even every month."

"Ashley mentioned that while I was waiting for you. It sounds like a pretty big deal."

"The biggest," he says and picks up his coffee cup again. "It's the biggest opportunity I've had since I started the business." He pauses to take a sip of his drink and then glances at me briefly. "What else did she say?"

My cheeks heat a bit recalling our conversation, which I am absolutely *not* going to tell Cole about. "Just stuff."

He chuckles. "Stuff. Hmm. I know what she's like so I can only imagine what that *stuff* was."

Cole lifts his Starbuck's cup to his lips, but glances over to me at the same time, pinning me with a stare I don't want to look away from. He brings the steaming cup from his mouth and a small smile tugs at the corner of his lips. God, I want to kiss those lips again.

He glances back to the street and—

"Shit!" Cole slams on the brakes and moves both hands to the steering wheel, dropping his coffee cup into his lap. The cup falls at an angle and the top hits the steering wheel. The lid comes off and coffee sprays all over Cole's lap.

The Jeep slams to a stop inches from the bumper of the car in front of us, and my seatbelt digs into my chest. My hands instinctively fly out in front of me.

"Fuck, that's hot!" Cole yells and then immediately directs his attention to me. "Are you okay?"

His hand is on my thigh as if to make sure I'm still there and even though sex should be the last thing on my mind right now, the skin underneath my jeans heats under his touch.

"I'm okay," I say in a breathy voice that probably gives away where my perverted thoughts are. "How about you?" I nod to his soaked shirt and jeans.

"Not gonna lie, this coffee is a little hot, but I think I'm okay."

"Are you sure?"

"Yeah, but do you mind if we swing by my place so I can change before we hit the next spot? We're not too far."

"Of course, of course."

We make the drive over to Cole's and every block that brings us closer makes me more and more nervous. The only time I've ever been to his house was the night I met him.

Will I walk through the door of his condo and have every action come rushing back to me and if so how will I handle that? With complete mortification or will it make me want him even more? I know myself well enough to know that I won't feel indifference.

He pulls the Jeep up a few yards from his place and takes the only empty parking spot on the street.

"Come on up so you don't have to wait in the car," he says.

I swallow past the lump in my throat. Time to put my big-girl panties on and find out.

# chapter
# TWENTY-TWO

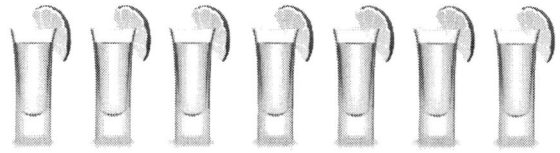

*I* WALK THROUGH THE door to Cole's place and . . . nothing.

Not one memory rushes forward. Much to my disappointment.

Cole leads me to the comfy-looking living room. "Make yourself comfortable. I'll just be a few minutes."

"Okay, thanks."

He heads to his room and I step into the living area. I don't take a seat on the broken-in brown leather couch because I'm too jittery to relax. Every surface I look at I wonder if Cole pinned me up against that wall and kissed me, or was this couch where he made me come with his hand?

I stand there pressing my thighs together to ease my building need while I envision all the embarrassing acts that may or may not have happened.

"You haven't told me anything else about that night," I call out before I can stop myself. "You still owe me today."

Cole's heavy footsteps sound on the hardwood flooring and he comes around the corner from the hallway I know leads to his bedroom.

"Would you like me to tell you or *show* you?" He cocks an eyebrow.

My mouth drops open at both his words and the visual in front of me. He's already removed his wet clothes, but hasn't bothered to get dressed yet and so he stands before me wearing only tight, black boxer briefs. Tight, black boxer briefs that do nothing to hide the large erection straining the cotton. There's no doubt in my mind that he prefers to *show* me exactly what went down that night.

I'm still standing there taking him in as he closes the distance between us. "Well, what will it be?" His voice has a low timbre that I can somehow *feel*.

"Did we have sex that night?" I have to know. I have to. Because if I slept with this man and don't remember it . . .

"No. We didn't." He steps closer toward me and if I reach out an inch I can run my hands down his toned abs. God, I want to feel those hard ripples so bad. "Not for lack of you trying, though."

I tilt my head a bit. "What does that mean?"

"It means you were drunk, horny, and intent on having your way with me. You got your hands on my unicorn cock—your words not mine—but once I realized just how drunk you were I put a stop to things and tucked you into bed. Hardest fucking thing I've had to do in a long time, believe me. I didn't want you waking up in the morning and regretting anything that happened between us."

The girly part of me swoons and the womanly part of me simmers.

There is so much more to this man than I could have ever guessed. After what happened years earlier, I'd pegged him as a rich snob who was used to getting his way and slept with any-thing in a skirt. Now I realize that he works hard and doesn't rest on his laurels. He has goals he wants to achieve and he feels things . . . deeply, if the hurt I saw in his eyes when he spoke about his father is any indication.

The most disconcerting part of it all is that every new piece of him I've discovered, I like.

A lot.

More than a lot, actually.

The only thing I don't know is what he's like as a lover. And I'm determined to rectify that right now. I'm tired of being afraid of what he makes me feel.

"I'm glad that nothing happened between us that night," I say and finally reach forward to run my fingertips over the muscles in his abs.

Cole sucks in a breath and his stomach muscles flex under the pads of my fingers.

"It would have been a shame for me not to remember it." I flick my gaze up to his eyes and he's watching my every move like a predator about to pounce. Never have I enjoyed being the prey so much.

"I could have filled you in on every detail." He sends one hand diving into my hair and pulls me into him, pressing my breasts against his hard chest.

"As much as I enjoy the sound of you talking dirty, I think I'd prefer if you show me all the things that didn't happen that night."

Cole growls and then fuses his lips to mine. I don't resist. Our tongues meet in a frenzy and I wrap my arms around him, enjoying the play of the muscles on his back as his hands explore my body.

He nibbles on my bottom lip and his mouth traces a path along my jawline and down onto my neck. I moan and allow my head to fall back to grant him more access. When I push my hands into his hair and pull, he groans and lightly bites my earlobe.

"That first night you came here there's a lot of things I didn't get to do that I wanted to," he says against my neck as he continues to drive me wild, dragging his tongue along my skin.

"Like what?" I pant.

He pulls back and stands to his full height, his hazel eyes taking me in, devouring me.

"I didn't do this." He reaches forward and grabs the collar of the thin shirt I'm wearing and rips it off me.

And by that, I mean he rips it right down the middle, leaving it hanging open, exposing my white lace push-up bra. It's a caveman act that soaks my panties.

I guess caveman is my thing.

I scramble to push the fabric off my arms and then reach back and unfasten my bra, letting it slide down my arms until it's puddled on the floor with my shirt.

His gaze dips to my tightened nipples and his hands cover each breast—squeezing and tracing his thumbs over my nipples.

"I didn't get to do this," he says, bending down and sucking one of them into his mouth, swirling his tongue around and around. My hand comes to the back of his head and I grip his hair.

He moves to my other nipple and this time he clamps down with his teeth until pain spikes in my chest, only to be swept away when he drags his tongue across it over and over.

Cole drops to his knees in front of me and begins to remove my shoes and socks, then undoes my jeans—pulling them down my legs until I'm almost naked in front of him, in only my sheer, wet panties.

"I've waited way too long to see you like this again, Whit. I feel like a starving man who's just come across a buffet." His focus veers back to my eyes. "I plan to eat my fill." His hand drops to his thick erection and he squeezes himself through his boxer briefs.

Aside from him ripping my shirt in half that might be the single most erotic thing I've ever seen in my life. I'll be reliving this moment for weeks to come.

Unable to stop myself, I reach up and squeeze both of my breasts. Cole's heavy-lidded gaze takes in every one of my movements as he continues to rub his hard cock.

"You're going to fucking kill me." His hand dips under the cotton of his boxer briefs and he strokes himself faster. "Keep touching yourself while I make you scream."

It's a promise, not a threat, and I hadn't thought it possible but my panties grow even damper than before. I am primed and ready for him and I don't feel like I can wait much longer to feel him inside me.

I continue fondling myself and Cole roughly yanks my underwear down my legs, his patience and self-control on the brink. His tongue trails a path all the way up to my neck again and he's standing before me when he takes my hand and leads me to the bedroom.

"On the bed," he says and nods his head in that direction.

He doesn't have to tell me twice. I crawl across the bed on my hands and knees, giving him a bit of a show by swaying my hips side to side a little more than necessary.

When I turn and lie down on my back he's pushing his hands through his hair and looking like he's trying to muster up some restraint.

I wish he wouldn't. I *want* to see him completely animalistic.

I lie there with my hands above my head and watch as he pushes his boxers down over his hips. They fall to the ground and he steps out of them, but all I can think of is how perfect this man is. How perfect his cock is. Long and thick and firm with the perfect vein running up the underside. Like a work of art.

He really is a unicorn cock.

While I'm busy taking him in he's doing the same and

reaches down and strokes himself a few times. I press my thighs together to ease the pressure because holy shit, I could come just watching him.

"You have no idea how many times I pictured this exact fucking scene," his raspy voice says, pulling my vision to his eyes. "And never was it as perfect and inviting as this." He strokes himself lightly and my gaze dips to his straining erection again while I lick my lips. I'm eager to taste him and drive him as crazy as he's making me right now.

But I don't get the chance because before I know it he's crawling across the mattress, using his hands to spread my legs, and positioning his shoulders between my legs.

"I definitely didn't get to do this that night." His thumbs spread me and he runs his tongue from my entrance all the way up to my clit. One of my hands dives into his hair and the other one grips the iron railing of the headboard above my head.

Cole laps at me again and again until I'm a writhing mess.

"I had no idea you'd taste so sweet, Whit." His eyes lock with mine over my mound while his tongue traces lazy circles over my clit. He sucks it into his mouth and my hips arch up and I moan, the feeling too intense.

His large hand pushes me back down to the mattress and I whip my head back and forth, not sure I can hold off my orgasm much longer. I'm on the brink when Cole pulls away and the hand I had in his hair drops to the bed.

My eyes spring open and I give him a questioning gaze.

"I want you to sit on my face. Switch places with me."

I don't even have a second to make sense of what he's saying before he takes my hand and helps me into a seated position. He takes the spot I was just in, lying with his back to the mattress, one hand behind his head. My eyes focus on his straining erection.

I could hop on right now and take what I really need, what I really want. As if he can read my mind he says, "Plenty of time for that later, sweetheart." He extends his hand out to me. "Now come here."

I take his hand and shimmy myself until I'm all the way up at the top of the mattress next to his head. Cole's licking his lips when I glance down at him. For a split second I'm nervous because I've never done this, but then I take in the expression on Cole's face—the pure lust, the abundance of need—and I know I have nothing to worry about.

"Now straddle me until you come on my face."

I do as he says, lowering myself tentatively down, not wanting to suffocate him, but Cole is having no part of that. Both his hands grip my hips and he pulls me down until his face is pressed into my pussy.

He flicks his tongue back and forth over my clit a few times, hard enough that I can feel it, yet light enough that I'm writhing for more.

I grip onto the headboard in front of me and moan when he straightens his tongue and starts fucking me with it.

*Oh. Oh, God.*

Why have I never done this before? Because this is fan-fuck-ing-tastic.

Eventually he moves back to my clit, sucking it into his mouth as one of his fingers slowly enters me, and then another. His other hand reaches up and twists my nipple between his finger and thumb.

I circle my hips as if I'm riding his cock.

When he arches his finger to hit my g-spot I'm a panting, quivering mess, so close to finishing.

"Come for me, Whit. Come all over my face." He pulls my clit back into his mouth and sucks hard while increasing the pressure on my nipple.

His words are my undoing and I throw my head back, ex-ploding into a million pieces, coming with a loud cry and jerking my hips back and forth to ride out my orgasm.

Cole is just as insatiable underneath me, lapping up my release until my quivering subsides.

I adjust myself back a bit and let my head fall forward to meet his gaze.

"We'll be doing that again," he says with a cocky grin. "But first I need to fuck you."

I simply nod, still in la-la land after my orgasm and unable to articulate any words. He helps me get off him and I lie sated on the bed, watching as he rolls over to his night table and pulls out a condom from the drawer.

He lies back and expertly rolls it over his hard cock and then rises to his knees on the mattress.

"I hope you weren't hoping for slow and gentle right now, because I'm going to make you scream until the police are kicking my door down."

I nod, hoping Cole is a man of his word.

# chapter
# TWENTY-THREE

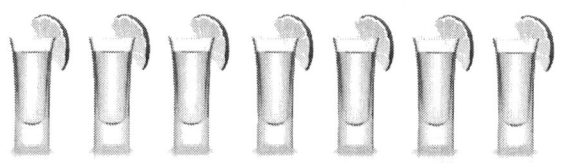

"**H**ANDS AND KNEES. ASS out," Cole orders.

I do as he says, wanting—no, *needing*—to feel him move inside me. My skin is on fire and my pussy throbs in anticipation.

He runs his hand over my ass cheeks a couple of times. "You make me want to do naughty, naughty things to you." He pushes two fingers in, drawing a moan out of me. I let my forehead fall to the mattress and close my eyes, basking in the sensation of the steady rhythm he's set.

Cole eventually pulls his fingers from me and trails them up toward my ass. He circles my puckered hole a few times and my breath hitches.

"Relax, sweetheart. We'll save that for another time. Right now I wanna be balls deep inside that sweet pussy of yours until I make you scream."

With one hand on my hip he lines himself up at my entrance and slowly pushes inside me. I release all the air in my lungs in relief. He holds himself there until I grow accustomed to his size.

I wiggle my hips a little, needing the delicious friction he's capable of. He takes the hint and groans as he pulls out of me.

The sound is deep and raspy and I turn my head to look at him. His head is thrown back in ecstasy and his eyes are closed. He pushes in again slowly one more time, setting every one of my nerves on fire. I let my head drop to the mattress as he leaves me and then, as if he's lost all control, he slams back into me.

I cry out in equal parts pleasure and surprise and it only ignites the fire within him more. He leans over my back and grabs both of my breasts in his hands, using them as an anchoring point as he pounds in and out of me.

And I like it. I love that Cole is so turned on by me that he can't control himself.

The room is silent except for the sound of our sweat-soaked skin slapping against one another and the moans of pleasure echoing off the walls.

"I want to see your face when I make you come," Cole grinds out.

His chest leaves my back and one of his hands dives into the hair at the back of my head, pulling so that my neck is arched back and I'm almost looking at him upside down.

"That's better," he says.

The sight of his chiselled, sweaty chest and the way he's looking at me like he could devour each and every piece of me has me working hard to stave off my orgasm.

He continues to drag his thick cock in and out of me and I know I won't be able to hold off much longer. Cole must recognize this because he shifts what he's doing with his hips so that he's driving into me at a different angle and oh, my God. He's hitting a spot inside me I didn't know existed and it's pure bliss.

Every part of my body tightens in anticipation of the coming release until I'm strung so tight I burst. My orgasm washes over me hard and fast and I burst like a confetti bomb, crying out Cole's name and a whole lot of gibberish that you won't find in the English dictionary.

"That's it, sweetheart. Come all over my cock." He holds himself deep inside me for a minute as I contract around him.

The orgasm rolls on forever and when I finally begin to ride the slow wave down from my high Cole releases my hair and my face drops to the bed.

Never have I ever come without my clit being involved. Ever.

Cole and his unicorn cock are like a gift from the Gods.

He grips my waist with both hands and drives into me a few more times, his efforts less coordinated now until he pulls all the way out. He must rip off the condom because seconds later his cock is riding the space between my ass cheeks and a warm substance hits the crest of my ass.

Cole groans and jerks against my skin a few more times before stilling behind me.

He marked me and it doesn't feel dirty, it feels right. This whole thing between us is feeling inevitable and destined.

The familiar fear of giving someone that kind of power over me creeps into my chest.

No. I will not go down that road right now.

*Not everyone will leave you. Not everyone will disappoint you.*

It's a mantra I've repeated many times when shit gets too real for me and I feel myself wanting to pull away.

Thing is, I don't know if I could pull away at this point even if I tried. I'm in too deep.

# chapter
# TWENTY-FOUR

COLE TOSSES THE WASHCLOTH he grabbed to help clean me up into his laundry hamper and joins me on the bed.

"That was even better than I imagined," he says and lies on his back, pulling me into his side. His hard chest is warm beneath my cheek.

"You've been imagining it, have you?" I ask with a chuckle.

"Haven't you?"

I glance up at him and he has an eyebrow arched, looking down at me.

"I'll never tell," I say in a singsong voice.

His arm tightens and he squeezes me closer to him and laughs. "Full disclosure—I've been jerking off thinking about what it would feel like to be buried inside you ever since that night you came home with me."

My cheeks heat and I squirm a little because the vision of him pumping his cock with his hand while thinking about me . . . damn. It makes me want to jump on his lap right now and ride him until we're both completely spent.

"Are you blushing?" Cole says with amusement. He cranes his neck back a bit to gain a better look at me.

"What? No." I tuck my face further into his chest. The inherently male scent of him—dried sweat and sex—makes me inhale deeper.

"You are." He laughs some more and tries to get me to dislodge my face from him by tickling me under the arms. "The girl who carries a vibrator around in her purse is embarrassed to know that I beat off to thoughts of her?"

Now he's just goading me for a reaction.

He somehow manages to slip his fingers under my armpit even though I'm squeezing my arms together as tight as I can. I turn over onto my back and he's above me, tickling me relentlessly while I scream and jerk and beg for mercy.

The sound of my cell phone ringing from my purse in the living room interrupts our fun.

"I have to get"—I squeal and try to get out from under him—"that. It could be one of my grandparents."

Cole lets his hands drop and tsks me. "Don't figure on being so lucky next time." He winks and it's charming, not cheesy, because it's Cole.

I slip from the bed and strut across the room to the bedroom door, naked.

"Nice view."

I smile to myself as I leave the room in search of my purse. I've never been an overly confident person. At least not to the point that I've been comfortable walking around in the nude in front of my exes. But Cole makes me feel wanted and desired so much that it doesn't feel like that big of a deal with him.

I spot my purse on the coffee table as another ring lets out. I rush over, grab my phone from inside, and hit the button to answer without taking a second to see who it is.

"Hello?"

"Hey! I'm so sorry it's taken me this long to get back to you."

It's Tahlia and though I'd normally be thrilled to hear from my best friend, her timing couldn't be worse. Her voice is like a pin to the balloon that holds my happiness and it deflates and I crash back down to earth.

"That's okay. I know you're busy."

"Still, that's no excuse. You've been so wonderful to go and tour all these places for me and run around town with a guy you couldn't care less for and I can't even take two seconds to get back to you. How's it going with Cole anyway? Have you killed each other yet?"

Oh, no. I'm not ready to tell her. I don't even have any idea what Cole and I are. We've slept together, yeah, but I imagine Cole sleeps with a lot of people. Do I mean something to him or am I a one-off and it's never going to happen again?

Taking the chicken route, I give her a routine answer that doesn't say much. "We're making it work. I don't want you to worry about us. Anyway, how was your trip?"

Tahlia rambles on about what a shit show it was when she arrived at the out-of-state plant and how she had to stay longer than expected to sort it all out. I guess she knows how to handle her meat.

I should explain. Tahlia's family owns the largest sausage company.

Yep. Sausages.

And before you make the obvious jokes, believe me when I say that Lennon has probably beat you to the joke at some point throughout the years. No surprise there, right?

After Tahl's done bitching about her job—one she's never really loved, but has always felt obligated to do—we move on to discuss all the venues.

"We were supposed to visit the last place on the list today,"

I say, my eyes lingering down the hallway, "but something came up."

*Cole's cock.*

"No worries. I appreciate you helping me this much as it is. And I think you're right, from what you've said it sounds like the Bentley Reserve is the place. I'll book an appointment to get in there and check it out for myself."

"I think you'll really like it there."

"Okay, I have to run. Chase didn't answer my calls when I got off the plane and I need to track him down so we can make some decisions on the list of stuff the wedding planner sent over."

"Sounds fun."

"This woman, I swear, Whit. I could run circles around her and do such a better job, but I barely have time for my manicures these days. Anyway, thanks for all your help. The three of us need to do drinks soon, all right?"

It takes me a second to realize that she means Lennon as the third party and not Cole.

"Um . . . yeah. Of course."

"Okay, I'll figure out when I'm free and we'll make it happen. Ciao for now."

The dial tone sounds in my ear and I drop my phone back into my purse. I stand there for a second chewing on the inside of my cheek, feeling like a terrible friend. I should have just told her when she called, but how can I do that when Cole is a room away and can probably hear every word I say?

Tahlia would bring up all my reasons for hating him from years ago. Beyond him ditching our blind date, he doesn't know what else happened that night. And I'm not ready to bring us down from the high we're both on. Either he'll think I'm insane for pinning any of the blame on him, or he'll feel bad about the repercussions.

Nope. I can't tell Tahlia until I know for sure what we are.

And the same goes for Cole.

After the mental pep talk, I head back into the bedroom.

Cole is on his back with both arms behind his head. The sheet is drawn up over him, but it's resting a few inches lower than his navel, covering all the best parts from my viewing pleasure.

"Is this the part where reality intrudes on our happy bubble?" he asks.

I exhale and join him under the covers. "That was Tahlia."

"I made that much out from what I was able to eavesdrop."

I smile then arrange myself beside him and prop myself up on my elbow. "She just arrived back in town."

He nods but doesn't speak. I get the feeling that he's letting me take the lead.

"I don't think we should say anything about what happened between us." I glance down to where I'm fiddling with his crisp, white sheets, unsure whether he's going to be offended or not.

"What's happening."

I raise my head and give him a questioning look.

"You said 'what happened' as if it was a one-time thing. Past tense. You should have said 'what's happening' because there's no way we aren't doing *that* again."

His words send a thrill through me—both physical and emotional. "Oh, really?" I tease.

"Count on it." He lifts his far hand out from under his head and trails a fingertip down the column of my neck and across to my shoulder blade. My nipples tighten in response underneath the sheet, something he doesn't miss.

"So you're in agreement? We won't tell them? This is probably something we should've talked about before, but . . ."

"You are too damn edible." He waggles his eyebrows and I laugh. "Anyway, sure. If you want to keep this between us I'm game."

"Thanks." And I mean it. Both for myself, because I'm a

chickenshit and don't want to tell my friend that I'm sleeping with her almost-brother-in-law, and for Tahlia, who doesn't need any more stress in her life right now.

"Was she happy with our efforts?" He shifts to face me, mimicking my position with his head propped up on his hand.

"She seemed to be. Sounds as if she's liking the look of the Bentley Reserve."

"That place was pretty cool." He pauses for a moment like he's remembering something and smiles to himself. The twelve-year-old girl inside me is hoping it's when I walked down the stairs and we shared a moment. "How come Tahlia was gone so long? Hard time pulling the sausage out?"

I laugh. "She didn't say exactly. Just mentioned that it took longer than she thought to figure it all out."

"I'm disappointed in Chase. You'd think he'd teach his woman how to massage meat." He smirks and I giggle like a schoolgirl that hasn't heard every sausage joke. "Speaking of sausages"—here comes another cheesy joke—"there's one in particular I'd like to show you." Cole wraps his arm around me and rolls over so his weight is pressed along my entire body while he hovers above me. And what delicious weight it is. The thin sheet is doing nothing to hide his own large . . . sausage.

Sorry, I couldn't help myself.

I laugh as he purposely digs his erection into my thigh.

"Chase must have been lonely with Tahlia out of town this long. Have you seen him much?" I ask in an effort to keep this conversation from devolving into double entendres.

"No, he's been hard to get a hold of." Something dark passes over his face, but it's gone before I can question it.

"That's what Tahl said. She had to let me go because she was trying to track him down." I chuckle but Cole's lips remain tightly closed.

"Enough about those two. I'm much more interested in

reacquainting you to my own grade-A sausage."

Without another word he leans in and kisses me, leaving all those warning signs that I should have paid attention to in my rearview mirror. All I see ahead of me is me, Cole and our hot naked skin grinding against each other.

You see, folks, denial isn't just a river in Egypt. It also has an outpost right here in San Francisco.

# *chapter*
# TWENTY-FIVE

A COUPLE OF WEEKS pass and autumn takes a firmer grip on the Bay area. I pull the zipper of my coat all the way up to my chin to stay warm as I stroll with Cole through Golden Gate Park.

Sparky's here, too. It's hard to forget him what with the constant pulling on the leash and yipping at every bird that dares to get within one hundred yards of us.

"Good news," Cole says and squeezes the hand I have interlocked with his. "I was finally able to secure an appointment with that distributor."

"No way!" Sparky picks up on my excitement and turns to face us on the path and barks. "That's awesome. When is it?"

"Not for a couple of weeks, but I'm excited. I think this could be my big break."

Pride fills my chest. Cole has been working so hard to make this happen. He's kept me apprised of all his efforts while I've been over at his place almost every night.

"Soon Rock Hard Whiskey will be in every bar from here to New York." I grin, unable to contain my excitement.

"Here's hoping." He exhales a big breath and I notice his nervousness for the first time. I've never seen his usual confidence wane, but it's a cute look for him.

I squeeze his hand and we begin walking again. "It will all work out."

We walk in contented silence for another minute when Sparky veers off the path to the grass and assumes the position. You know the one—the one that tells you to get your little plastic baggy ready.

"This is the worst part of having a dog by far. Even more annoying than the fact that he ruined another pair of my shoes last week."

Cole chuckles and we both stop and wait for the little fur ball to do his business.

My phone rings from inside my cross-body bag. I drop Cole's hand and pass him the leash. "Do you mind?"

He takes it while I search for my phone. I come upon the plastic baggy first so I pass it to Cole with a pleading expression. He takes it, reluctantly.

"You're going to owe me one," he teases.

I blink my eyelids fast in a girly fashion and he shakes his head. Finally, I find my phone and hit the green button and bring it up to my ear.

"Hello?" I say.

"Hi, is this Whitney Knight?" I'm not sure who it is but the woman has a professional tone that tells me this isn't a telemarketer call.

"This is she."

"Hi, Whitney, this is Marla from Human Resources at WHFI."

I turn away from Cole and Sparky and begin pacing in a small circle on the path. "Hi, Marla."

"Unfortunately, I'm calling to let you know that the

producers and Mr. Jeffries have made a decision about the job you applied for and have decided to offer the position to a different candidate."

Disappointment, heavy and swift, finds a home inside me and I stop pacing. "Oh. I'm sorry to hear that."

"Rest assured we'll keep your résumé on file should anything else come up." It's clear from her tone that she's made a thousand of these calls in her lifetime. Everyone knows that 'keeping your résumé on file' means that it goes to die in some forgotten box in an office no one uses anymore.

"Thank you for calling," I say, not really meaning it.

"My pleasure. You have a good day."

"You, too."

She hangs up on her end and I let my hand drop from my ear.

My back is to Cole and I don't want to turn around. I know there's no way I'll ever be able to hide the disappointment and desperation I feel.

"Is everything okay?" he asks with genuine concern in his voice.

I suck in a deep breath through my nose and turn to face him, blinking back the tears in my eyes. "That was the lady from the TV station. I didn't get the job."

He steps forward and pulls me into his chest. We wrap our arms around each other and he squeezes me tight. "I'm so sorry, Whit. Something will come along. You're beautiful and intelligent. It's going to happen."

I bury my face in his chest and allow myself to enjoy the feel of his strong body, the scent of his cologne, and his words of comfort.

I'm not accustomed to letting anyone support me and I realize that as much as I don't want to, as much as I want to be the girl who doesn't need anyone, this feels nice and safe and . . . right.

"Don't worry, sweetheart. It'll all work out." He runs his hand up and down my back.

"Thanks," I say in a quiet voice, not sure I believe him.

After another minute of shellacking myself to his chest, I pull away. Cole frames my face with his hands. "I want to take you out on a proper date."

As much as I love the sound of that, I have my concerns. Since we became whatever we are, we've mostly just hung out at Cole's place because I don't want to chance running into anyone we know. The only reason we're able to hang out here in the park is because neither Cole's brother or my best friend are exactly the outdoorsy types.

"I know what you're thinking and don't worry." He brushes a hand over my hair. "I'm not going to take you anywhere Chase and Tahlia would ever dare to go."

"You don't have to do that, Cole. I'll be fine." *After a few pints of Ben & Jerry's buried in a bottle of wine.*

"I know I don't have to, I want to."

As depressed as I am, I wouldn't mind some wooing right now. "Okay then."

He leans down and gives me a chaste kiss on the lips. Sparky barks and begins tugging on his leash again. That dog has no appreciation for public displays of affection.

"All right, little guy. Cool your jets."

We continue through the park, hand in hand, and though the disappointment of not getting the job eats away at me, the pain is tempered, at least in part, by the company I keep.

⟶⟶⟶

FROM THE MOMENT WE arrived down at the Pier, Cole made me promise to keep my eyes closed and led me by hand to our destination. The sound of people wandering past filters into my ears as I stand here, positioned just so by Cole, his hands covering my eyes from behind me.

"Promise you won't laugh," Cole says as he slides his hands away from my eyes.

I blink for a second, adjusting my eyesight to the scene before me.

"A maze of mirrors . . ." I smile slowly.

"I thought you could use some fun to get your mind off everything."

The job. He means the job, because besides Cole himself that's the only thing I've been able to focus on these past few days—the fact that I let the job of my dreams somehow slip through my hands.

"I never would have guessed this."

"That was the point." He leans down and kisses me before taking my hand to lead me inside the building.

Loud music is playing inside, some newer song I've heard on the radio a few times. The carpet on the floor has a crazy pattern made up of black, blue, red, and yellow and a fresh-faced teenage girl stands behind the counter smiling over at us.

"Welcome to the Maze of Mirrors," she says and we make our way over to her.

"Hi there. I'm Cole Webber."

"Oh, yes, Mr. Webber. We've been expecting you." The way she smiles at Cole all dreamy-eyed tells me he'll be a focal point of her diary entry tonight. I stifle a chuckle so as not to embarrass her.

"I should already be paid up. I took care of everything over the phone with the manager."

"You are. The place is all yours."

I give Cole a questioning look.

"I may not be my brother, but I know when to use my

money and influence for good," he says and leans in closer to my ear so that only I can hear him over the music pumping out of the overhead speakers. "And if it means using it to rent this place out to ourselves so that I can get you alone instead of being surrounded by a hundred shithead teenagers, I'm gonna do it."

He pulls back and my heated stare meets his. We each take in the promise of what it is we'd like to be doing to the other one right now.

"The lockers are to your right if you'd like to put your jackets in there, Mr. Webber."

We both turn our attention to the young girl and a giggle escapes my lips at how she keeps calling him Mr. Webber. I'm not sure why I find it so funny, but it just doesn't suit the man I've come to know.

He helps me off with my coat and puts both of ours in the rented locker and comes to stand beside me, taking my hand in his. This small gesture fills me with a warmth and security that I don't want to examine too much.

"What's the fastest anyone has ever made it out of the maze?" Cole asks.

"Twelve minutes and thirty-seven seconds," she says. Her chin is nudged up a bit and her chest is puffed out as if she's very proud that she knows this information.

"Shall we see if we can beat that?" Cole asks with a grin.

"Definitely."

He begins to direct me toward the door that says 'Entry' above it and the young girl calls out behind us, "Have fun, Mr. Webber."

I full-on laugh this time as we push through the swinging doors. On the other side the music is just as loud but it's much darker and strobe lights flicker every so often. There's what appears to be thousands of arched columns ahead with mirrors between them and reflections of us from all different angles appear in all the glass.

"What are you laughing at?" Cole asks over the music.

"At that smitten kitten out there calling you Mr. Webber."

He pulls me into him and I immediately heat at the feeling of his hard body pressed into my soft curves.

"It's my name, isn't it?"

I nod. "But somehow it doesn't really fit. I've heard people call your brother Mr. Webber before and thought nothing of it, but it seems almost comical to hear someone refer to you that way."

Cole tilts his head a bit, and places his thumb on my bottom lip. "I'm going to take that as a compliment."

"Good." I push up on my tippy toes and place a kiss on his lips. "It was meant as one."

He grins. "As long as we're clear."

"Are we going to conquer this bad boy? We'd better get going if we're going to beat the record."

Almost reluctantly he pulls away, takes my hand once again, and we head into the insanity to see if we can navigate our way out.

WE DON'T HOLD HANDS for long. You need both of your hands out in front of you, as Cole discovers when he walks head first into what we thought was empty space between columns, but is really a mirror.

The maze is so disorienting. It's hard to know what's real and what's not and it's near impossible to keep track of which way you've come and which direction you're heading. It reminds me a lot of my life lately.

Everywhere you look there appears to be more than one of us. We can see ourselves from so many different angles and I've been taking full advantage—watching on as Cole's expressions change, the way the muscles in his arms bunch and flex under the fabric of his thin, maroon Henley shirt, how his ass moves when he takes a step forward. Being able to see all that multiple times from multiple angles without him knowing has been amazing.

In fact, it's got me wanting to do things that seem more up Lennon's alley, but something about this man makes me lose my inhibitions and throw aside the part of me intent on self-preservation.

"Another dead end." Cole laughs.

Instead of turning back and heading the way we came, I don't move when Cole turns around from the sheet of glass in front of him to face me. Rather, this time I nudge his shoulders until his back is pressed up against the glass.

His expression looks bemused until he registers the heat in my gaze. Without a word, I circle his neck with my arms and drag his face down to mine.

Our tongues meet in a passion-filled clash of primal instinct, and after a minute it feels as if my lips are bruised. Not in a painful way, but in a way that assures I'll be reliving this moment for days.

I snake my hand down Cole's body until I'm gripping his hard length pressing through his jeans. He groans into my mouth and my knees weaken. I close our kiss, knowing if I don't stop, I'll miss my opportunity, and then I drop to my knees in front of him.

I tilt my head up and look at him through my lashes. His chest is heavy with his efforts at breathing. "What are you doing?" He's loud enough so I can hear him over the music.

I raise a brow. "Exactly what you're hoping I'm doing."

My eyes never veer away from him as I undo his belt buckle, the button on his jeans, and then pull the zipper down. His large cock is straining the cotton of his white boxer briefs. When I pull the elastic down a bit his cock springs free and I arrange his underwear so it sits tucked under his balls.

Since I first saw his cock I've wondered what Cole tasted like. I've imagined the way his hands would thread into my hair when I sealed my lips around the head. How he'd moan when he breached the back of my throat.

I'm about to rock his world and cement myself in his memory for an eternity. Sometimes it pays to have a friend like Lennon—you inevitably learn some skills just by listening to her absurd stories.

I lick my lips as I lean forward. My tongue traces lightly across his mushroom tip where a bead of pre-cum awaits. He sucks in a breath and holds it in for a moment, but once my tongue is back in my mouth, a slow stream of air flows out of his mouth.

Leaning in again, this time I run my tongue from the base of his length all the way to the top and back down the other side. Cole pushes his hands into my hair, and I raise my gaze to meet his. It's dark in here, but I can still see that his hazel eyes are heavy-lidded with lust, and his mouth hangs open.

I continue licking him all over again and again until his entire cock is wet with my saliva. I grip the bottom of his shaft with one hand and then lower my mouth to suck one of his balls in past my lips. Cole's hands twitch in my hair and grip the strands harder. Moans float out of his mouth while I suck gently and stroke up and down his length, twisting my hand near the top. His head thumps against the mirror behind him and he squeezes his eyes shut. His chest is rising and falling in an erratic rhythm and I've never been as high as I am right now from being the one who is unraveling him.

The power to drive him crazy makes me wild, horny, and needy. My nipples could cut granite and my clit is throbbing, begging for attention.

Right when Cole is on the edge of an orgasmic cliff I pull

back and wrap my lips around him, pushing forward until his tip hits the back of my throat.

"Oh, fuck, sweetheart."

Cole's hips push forward again and again and he sets his own pace. I glance up to meet his gaze, but he's not looking down at me. No, his gaze is wandering from one mirror to the next, taking in the image of me sucking him off from every available angle.

I shift a little so I can see us in the mirror, too.

Watching him push into my mouth and work himself into such a frenzy so that he's fucking my mouth is more erotic than the porno movie hidden in that secret file on my hard drive. Now, it's like I'm starring in my own porno. I'm watching the scene of 'Whitney and Cole getting it on in the mirror maze' as if I'm an outsider. It's never been more apparent to me just how crazy and insane I make this man.

Pride wars with need inside me. I want to watch as he empties himself into me and I swallow him down. I want to watch every minuscule expression on his face as he unglues into a muddled mess. I want to watch his ecstasy-filled eyes look at me like I'm the only girl for him.

"I'm gonna come," Cole pants out, giving me fair warning to back away. But I don't want to stop. The urge to know what he tastes like is a burning need inside me.

I cup his balls in my hand and squeeze lightly, pushing my lips all the way down to his base. He twitches in my mouth and releases a noise that sounds like a mix between a growl and a groan. Hot, salty liquid pours down the back of my throat while he jerks his hips in an off-rhythm way until he's completely spent.

I pull away and wipe my chin with the back of my hand. Cole extends a shaking hand to help me up and wastes no time in kissing me once I'm on my feet.

With tongue.

I love that he kisses me with tongue.

In the past, some of my exes have pulled their heads away in the same situation and it's always bothered me because after a guy eats you out he expects you to kiss him and to love the taste of yourself. It's a turn-on for them and I get it, but you have to be willing to return the favor. I can't stand sexual double standards.

After our kiss, he lowers his forehead to rest on my own while he tucks himself in and fastens his pants back up.

"You are something else, Miss Knight."

I grin. "Well, thank you, Mr. Webber."

"I'll be getting mirrors installed in my bedroom. On every surface."

I laugh.

"It's cute that you think I'm joking." He leans forward and places a chaste kiss on my mouth.

A thought occurs to me. "Do you think they have cameras in here?" My eyes widen.

"Honestly, I could care less. That was worth it even if they do."

"We probably just scarred that poor girl for life."

He chuckles.

"Should we work on finding our way out of here now? I'm curious to see what else you have planned for us tonight." I press myself against him, unable or unwilling to extract myself from the need to feel him.

"I think you're really going to like what I have planned next for us." He slips his hands into mine, intertwining our fingers.

"I don't doubt it."

And I realize I *don't* doubt him. For the first time in forever I'm not obsessing about keeping my independence and not allowing myself to get too close to a guy. I'm letting whatever might happen, happen. And to my surprise it feels way better than I thought it would.

*chapter*

# TWENTY-SIX

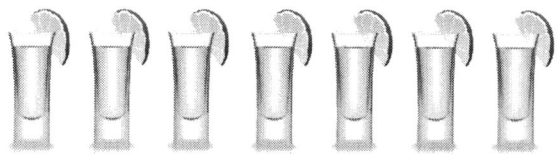

W E WALK INTO THE Ice Cream Bar and I'm immediately in love with the place. I glance over at Cole.

"Well, you had me at the name, but this place looks amazing!"

His grin widens. He's obviously pleased with himself for picking a good spot. But really, this place is too much.

It's a throwback to a 1930's-style soda fountain and lunch counter. The soda jerks behind the counter all wear crisp white shirts with a black bow tie, white aprons tied at the waist, and little white hats that harken back to another era.

There's a pair of seats available at the end of the counter and Cole nods in that direction. "Do you want to sit over there?"

"Absolutely." I shimmy onto the stool, remove my coat and purse, and set them on the very edge of the counter, out of the way. Cole passes me his coat and the scent of his cologne wafts by me as I place it on top of the pile.

I'm not sure I'll ever get enough of that smell. I'm not even sure if it's entirely his cologne or if it's his own natural scent, but whatever it is, it makes me wet. Scentsy needs to make that their new scent—Cole Webber's Orgasm Inducer.

He pulls a menu out of the metal prongs and passes one to me, then opens the other himself.

"What's good here?" I ask, then glance to my side when he doesn't answer right away.

His eyes trail down my body for a moment before he returns eye contact with me. "What I feel like eating right now isn't on the menu."

I press my lips together and blush. Then I smack his arm with the menu. "Behave," I scold.

He leans in and speaks directly into my ear. "Was that you behaving when you were on your knees with my cock in your mouth?"

I press my thighs firmly together. He eyes me shifting my ass on the vinyl stool and chuckles before leaning back from me.

I force myself to study the menu some more, eventually deciding on the PB&J, which probably seems silly, but seriously. Where else can you get a peanut butter and jelly sandwich at a restaurant? I have to try it.

"What can I get you kids?" The guy behind the counter approaches. I stifle a chuckle because I'm pretty sure he's about our age. Must be part of the whole soda jerk persona.

"I'm going to have the PB&J." I smile wide and Cole shakes his head.

"I'll have the pulled pork," Cole says.

"And to drink?" the waiter, whose nametag I now see says Ned, asks.

"They all look so good. I don't know how to decide," I say, because really, there's a bunch of variations of milkshakes, floats, and sodas on this menu, any and all of which sound mouthwatering.

"Why don't you try the Too Good to be True milkshake?" Cole offers.

"Why that one?" I ask, scanning the menu to read its ingredients.

He shrugs. "Seems fitting."

I glance up at Ned and I know my cheeks are stained pink. "Okay, let's go with that."

Ned nods. "And for you?"

"I'm going to go with the O Canada. I haven't tried that one yet and Canadians are always going on and on about how good their maple syrup is. Let's see if that's the case."

"Very good. I'll have the milkshakes over here in a few minutes."

We both thank him and then shoot the shit as we watch Ned, fascinated by him concocting our drinks. At least I'm fascinated.

I'm realizing making a milkshake is an art form. Almost like he's developing a potion. Cole explains to me that everything is made in-house and handcrafted. Even the sodas. There's no pouring a bottle of cola into a float. No, they use homemade syrups and tinctures and whatever else they need—shaking cream with an egg over ice to make the ice cream.

Color me impressed.

"For the lady." Ned sets my milkshake down in front of me and my mouth waters at the sight of it.

"Thank you." I waste no time, leaning in and placing my mouth around the straw, sucking hard to get the ice cream up the straw. When the cold, sweet liquid hits my tongue I close my eyes and a little moan escapes my throat and then I suck in some more.

It really is the best milkshake I think I've ever had. By the time I come back to myself and steal a glance over at Cole he's sitting staring at me with heavy-lidded eyes, his milkshake untouched.

"What?" I ask and sit up straighter in my chair, feeling a

little self-conscious.

He pushes his hand through his hair. "You."

I double-blink. "Me what?"

"You drinking that milkshake with your little noises and your lips wrapped around that straw. The way your cheeks are sucked in. And did I mention your lips? It's all a little distracting." He shifts in his chair and I get the impression he's doing it to try to hide something. Like a hard-on.

I chuckle. "You seem to be somewhat obsessed with my lips now, Mr. Webber."

He leans in further and I catch his scent. "Miss Knight, you have no idea just how obsessed I am."

I play off his comment, not knowing if he's talking about me in general, or my lips as a result of the killer blow job I gave him an hour ago. I don't want to read too much into his words, but it doesn't escape me the way my stomach did a somersault as a result of them.

Cole sucks some of his milkshake up his straw. "Mmm. Maybe Canadians are right. This is good." He takes another quick sip and slides it across the counter in my direction. "Want to try some?"

"Sure." I lean over and Cole's gaze is once again intent on my lips. A smile curves at the corner of my mouth as I taste his milkshake. "Wow. That is really good."

We each enjoy our sweet treats in silence for a few minutes before Cole pushes his away and turns on his stool to face me.

"I need to save some room for my meal," he says, patting his stomach.

"Good idea," I agree after I've taken another quick sip.

"Did you study journalism when you went to college?" Cole asks, catching me off guard.

"I was an English Lit major, but I was involved with the campus newspaper."

"That's got to be good for your résumé."

"I suppose." I shrug. Doesn't seem to have gotten me very far on my job search.

"Where did you say you went to school again?"

It's an innocent enough question, but I tense in my seat. The moment I've been worried about is here.

I can't pretend that what's happening between us is temporary or that we're simply bang buddies. I might not know exactly *what* this is, but I know what *I* want it to be. And for us to stand any chance at all I'm going to have to tell him what happened the night he ditched me all those years ago, and how I blamed him for the trajectory my life took.

"I ended up at Berkeley, but I was supposed to go to University of Nebraska."

A crease forms in his forehead. "Nebraska is a really good school. What happened?"

He must be able to tell that I'm uncomfortable because he reaches over and engulfs my hand in his much larger one, rubbing his thumb back and forth over my knuckles. The act is soothing and nice.

I draw in a deep breath and decide to rip the duct tape off. "Do you remember the night we were supposed to go on that blind date?" He nods, the crease in his forehead deepening. "After I spoke with you on the phone and I left the restaurant I was so mad. Fuming. It was getting dark and rather than take a cab home I decided to walk off some of the adrenaline running through my system. I was too preoccupied with what was going on in my head and wasn't watching my surroundings." Cole squeezes my hand and since I've been staring down at the counter while I tell this story, I finally look up and meet his gaze.

"About halfway home a man approached. He was right up in my space before I realized what was about to happen." I swallow past a lump in my throat as the memories come back. "Thank

God all he wanted was my purse, but instinct had me fighting him for it, which I know was stupid, but in the moment . . . I don't know. I didn't think, I guess. We fought and he ended up pushing me to the ground before running down the street. I landed funny and injured my shoulder. Could barely get up off the ground. I had to wait until someone else came down the street and they called an ambulance."

Cole's gaze drops from mine and he looks down at the black and white tiled floor. "Shit, Whit. I don't know what to say." He's frowning and shaking his head. "What does that have to do with you not going to Nebraska?" He lifts his head and the pained expression on his face takes me back a moment.

"I had a full scholarship to go to Nebraska and play volley-ball. The injury to my shoulder was bad enough that I would never be able to perform at the same calibre I was playing at and so they pulled my scholarship. I ended up going to Berkley by default, racking up student loans, and was never able to play at the collegiate level."

My words hang in the air between us.

I'm sure it's obvious, but in case it's not I need to get it all out. There's no point in doing this halfway.

"Cole, the reason I hated you so much was because I blamed you for what happened. I blamed you for the fact that I was never able to pursue my dream and for the fact that I left school buried in debt. I told myself that if you hadn't acted the way you had that night, I wouldn't have been on the street at that particular time, or if I was I would have been more aware of what was going on around me and I'd have seen that guy coming. I held you responsible for all of it."

He lets go of my hand and leans forward, dropping his head into his hands, not saying a word.

I'm not sure what to say and so I wait. And wait.

When he finally turns on his stool to face me he cups my

face in his hands. His eyes are full of guilt and sorrow.

"No wonder you hated me. I'm so, so sorry." He presses his lips together and sucks in a deep breath through his nose. "Why didn't you say anything sooner?"

I move my hand up to cover one of his. "I didn't know what to say. And then as I got to know you better I realized something . . . it *wasn't* your fault. It wasn't anyone's fault except the guy who mugged me."

"No, Whit, if I hadn't—"

"Stop. That's why I'm telling you now. Because I want you to know that spending time with you has taught me something."

"What could I have possibly taught *you*?" He looks on at me like he's hanging by a thread waiting for my answer.

"Sometimes things just happen—good and bad—for no other reason than they just do."

The hard lines of his face soften a bit and I'm hopeful that he'll be able to forgive himself the same as I've done.

"That's difficult to accept." I can see that he wants to believe me. Because if he can't it will be something that stands between us always. I know exactly how much those emotions that you push down can fester and grow until you've conjured up a whole story in your mind and it's hard to even remember why you felt that way in the first place.

"You *have* to accept it. You have to if you want this to continue." I let my hand drop and motion between the two of us.

He nods, though reluctantly. "I will never be the cause of you hurting like that again. Ever."

He leans in and his lips meet mine with a kiss infused with determination and promise. I melt into him and the thought crosses my mind that there's no longer anything else between us. It feels like I'm all in and rather than fear, all I can focus on is the amount of joy wanting to burst out of my chest.

# chapter
# TWENTY-SEVEN

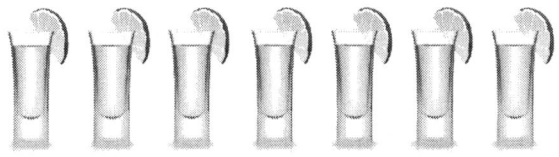

*I* PLOP MYSELF DOWN in the booth and slide over to make room for Tahlia. Lennon's sidled up to the bartender she flirted with the last time we were here, probably deciding between the storage room and alley.

"How are you doing?" I ask as I remove my jacket and place it between the wall and me. Tahlia takes off hers as well and hands it to me to do the same with hers.

"Was I crazy to think that planning my wedding was going to be more fun than this?"

We spent the day dress shopping with both Tahlia's and Chase's mothers. It was clear from the get-go that Mrs. Santora had some strong ideas about what type of dress would be suitable for Tahlia to wear to 'the wedding of the decade', or so her mom had dubbed it. Tahl and her mom clashed more than a few times over the course of the day.

"Everyone just wants the day to be perfect." I reach out and rub her back while she leans forward and places her head in her hands to massage her temples. "I'm sure once all the big decisions are out of the way everyone will relax a bit."

I say the words I don't believe. But hey, what are friends for if not to blow smoke up your ass when you need it?

"I'd say we could each use a little of this after today." Lennon slides a tray in front of us and crawls into the booth on the other side. The tray holds a drink for each of us and six shots.

To my surprise Tahl reaches forward for one of the shots and pours it down her throat, coughing and sputtering as she slams the empty shooter glass back down on the tray.

"That's awful. What is that?" she asks.

"Rock Hard Whiskey," Lennon replies with an evil smirk.

"Oh, that's Cole's little pet project. Did you know that?" Tahl asks her.

"I think someone must have mentioned it at some point. Sounds familiar."

That someone was me, of course. I know what Lennon's doing. I told her I was going to come clean with Tahlia about boinking her future brother-in-law. I'd planned to tell her after dress shopping, knowing we had plans to have a couple of drinks, but after the way the day went I'm second-guessing whether now is the right time.

"I don't think you're their target market, Tahl," I say.

"No, probably not." She stares at the empty shooter and spins it around and around, deep in thought.

Lennon removes her jacket and then the light, long-sleeve sweater she had on underneath. "It feels good to take that off. I was sweating like a fat man in a sauna at the dress shop, but I knew your mother would have a conniption if I showed my tats off in that place."

My eyes widen and my eyeballs almost burst out of my eye sockets when I see what's on her t-shirt. At the top of the shirt just above her breasts it says: WANTED and underneath there's a picture of a cartoon rooster leaning back with a satisfied grin on his face, only this rooster has a unicorn horn on its head, a pink horse tail and pink hair on top of its head. Underneath the cartoon are the words: APPLY WITHIN.

Tahl's face is scrunched up. "What the hell is that supposed to be?"

"A unicorn cock. Get it?" Lennon smiles wide. "Apply within?" She winks.

"I don't even know what that is," Tahlia says.

"It's the cock that ruins you for all other cocks. Right, Whit?" She's giving me those eyes like now is the perfect time to divulge my secret. Is she crazy? Wait. I already know the answer to that.

"Yeah, I guess." I reach forward and grab my own shot glass, downing it in one gulp. The taste reminds me of the night I met Cole and only serves to make me feel that much guiltier for not being forthcoming with Tahlia.

"Oh," Tahl says. "I wouldn't know." She's looking down at her hands on the table.

Lennon and I exchange a concerned glance and then look over to our friend.

"Is everything okay, Tahl?" I ask.

"Yeah, you don't exactly seem like the blushing bride these days," Lennon adds.

Tahlia reaches for one of the glasses and brings it to her mouth to take a sip. "I don't know. I mean, yes, everything is fine, it's just . . . I have so much pressure on me at work. And there's a million decisions to be made for the wedding. I thought Chase would be more hands-on than he has been and so everything is falling to me to handle. My mother . . . well, you know my mother. She's so concerned that I'm going to embarrass her by not choosing the right food, the right cake, or the right invitations. And the wedding planner she hired is making me batshit crazy. That old broad wouldn't know class if you hit her over the head with it. I mean, who suggests peach as the accent color for a wedding? It's not 1986. I have no idea how she came so highly recommended. I've just got a lot going on. I'm sure once all these decisions are out of the way I'll feel better about it all. It's just not how I pictured planning my wedding to be." She takes a deep breath and leans back in her seat, seeming to relax a little at being able to vent and get her frustrations all out.

Lennon and I are both quiet for a minute before we say anything. I think we're both in shock. I've never heard Tahlia speak so much at once.

"Maybe you should postpone the wedding," I offer. "So you have more time to get everything done."

Tahl gives a caustic laugh. "Are you kidding? Everyone knows it's supposed to be this spring. My mom would never allow it. People would think there's trouble between Chase and me."

I glance over at Lennon, urging her to say what I'm sure we're both thinking. She takes the hint.

"Is there *trouble* with you guys?"

Tahlia whips her head up, her eyes narrowing.

Lennon puts her hands up in a placating gesture. "I'm not implying there is. I'm only asking because you seem so stressed out lately and you've lost that la-la look you used to get on your face whenever you mentioned Chase."

"I don't know what you're talking about," Tahl responds and lifts her glass to take another drink.

"Please. If I put a cartoon of you on my shirt you'd be this wisp of a blonde thing with hearts in her eyes, her hands clenched to her chest."

Tahl's shoulders sag a bit before she leans back and crosses her arms over her chest.

"You know you can talk to us," I say, now really concerned that Lennon's hit on something here.

"Things are fine between us. When we see each other. Which isn't a lot these days. He's usually busy with his family's business, or I am. Or I'm trying to nail down decisions about the wedding that he doesn't seem all that interested in weighing in on. But that's probably normal, right?" She looks between Lennon and I with a hopeful expression. "I mean, what guy really wants to be involved in picking color schemes or which trim to cut the invitations in?"

"In my experience, just the gay ones," Lennon says.

A small smile plays on Tahl's lips.

"You two are just under a lot of pressure right now. You both have so much going on. I'm sure once this passes you'll be back to your usual selves." I reach forward and squeeze her hand.

"Yeah, you're right. Getting married is a lot of pressure for anyone, but with the two families we come from it's even worse. We just need to get through this planning stage and then we'll be good."

"Glad that dilemma is solved," Lennon says and then fires back a shot without flinching. "Now, I'm dying to know what you girls think of my Tickled Pink vibrator!"

Tahlia and I exchange a glance.

I'm not sure what to say because I haven't tried it. I can't get the image of Sparky with it between his teeth out of my head. The vision isn't exactly conducive to becoming aroused, but I can't bring up that entire fiasco in front of Tahl.

"You guys have tried it, right?" Lennon asks, her hands pressed to the table in front of her.

"I haven't yet. I'm sorry." I grimace as she shakes her head in mock disappointment at me. It's hard to get worked up over a vibrator with a dog's teeth marks in it.

"What about you, Tahl?" Lennon crosses her arms over her chest.

"I've been travelling and I'm not going to take something like that with me. What if security wants to search my luggage at the airport?"

I giggle because Tahlia looks beside herself at the thought.

"How am I supposed to improve my design and secure more investors if I can't tell people it's tried, tested, and true?"

"I promise I will give it a go this week, okay?" Tahl says.

I nod in agreement. I'll need to call Lennon on the side to let her know the fate of the pink sex toy she gave me.

"I want you each to report back." She raises her hand to catch the bartender's eye. When he looks over at us she holds up the empty shot glass and wiggles it side to side. Like a good bartender, he understands the non-verbal signal and winks at her before turning to grab some empty shot glasses from the shelf behind him.

"Did you ever sleep with him that night?" I ask.

"What night?" Tahlia asks.

"When you were out of town we came here for drinks and Lennon was determined to take him home."

Tahl nods, unaffected, because this is not an uncommon occurrence for our friend.

"Of course I did." Lennon takes a sip of her drink and sets it down. "Then I gave him that awesome tat you see on his forearm."

We both glance over and spot the tattoo in question as he's pouring liquid fire into a shot glass.

"Nice," I say. Not because we're friends but because Lennon is amazing at what she does.

"Well. How was it?" Tahlia asks.

Lennon shrugs. "Not bad. Eight out of ten. Worth repeating."

"I guess we'll have to make sure each other gets home okay tonight then," I say to Tahlia. "Sounds like Lennon's busy later."

"Here's hoping." Lennon raises her glass and we all follow suit. "May we get what we want. May we get what we need. But may we never get what we deserve."

We all laugh and clink our glasses together.

It's good to have some time with just the three of us. Even if the guilt I feel from keeping something from one of my best friends is eating away at the pit of my stomach.

After we've all taken a sip of our drinks and set them back down Tahl scoots out of the booth. "I have to go to the bathroom."

She's barely out of earshot before Lennon pounces.

"Are you still going to tell her about Cole?"

My eyes dart to the hallway that Tahlia just entered to make sure she's not headed back this way. "I don't see how I can. You heard her earlier. You *saw* her all day. I think she's at her breaking point. What do you think?"

Lennon runs her hands through her chin-length black hair and then fluffs it up a bit. "I hate the fact that we know something she doesn't, but with her state of mind right now I honestly don't know how she'd react."

I take a large swallow of my drink. "I don't want to be responsible for ruining what's supposed to be one of the happiest times in her life."

"Doesn't seem like that's the case anyway."

"I know. That's my point. I'm worried about her." I bite my bottom lip.

Lennon focuses on the glass she's spinning around in her hands before she answers. "Me, too."

"I think I should wait. She has some strong opinions about Cole. I'd be surprised if she was happy about the news."

"Fine. But you can't wait too long. Sooner or later it's going to come out and it'll be a thousand times worse if she finds out from someone other than you."

I nod, knowing she's right, but still feeling like I'm caught between two pieces of bread in a shit sandwich.

# chapter
# TWENTY-EIGHT

*I* LIE TANGLED IN Cole's bed sheets with one leg draped over his, my front pressed into his side, while we lazily watch *Game of Thrones*. We do a lot of this after we've had sex. Almost like we don't want to leave the scene of the crime—or the orgasm, as it were. Well, orgasms, plural.

"How are you feeling about your big meeting?" I ask.

"Good," he says, wiggling under me.

We've been counting down until the day that Cole meets with the national distributor and now that we're less than a week out he seems to be getting more and more nervous every time I bring it up.

"Do you think you're prepared?"

His fingertips brush up and down my upper arm a few times. "As much as I can be. I've got all my figures and projections pulled together. We've laid out a plan of how we're going to produce enough product, should we be successful and have to supply to bars and restaurants across the nation."

"Well, I for one think you are going to nail your meeting." I turn my head and press my lips to his chest for good luck. I don't think that's really a thing—kissing bare chests for good luck—but it totally should be. I'll take any excuse I can to get my lips on this man.

"Thank you. I hope you're right."

"Of course I am. I'm always right."

"Is that so?" He chuckles and the rich, deep sound reverberates through his chest into my ear. I smile.

Cole's hand trails a path down my arm, onto my hip and then dips between my legs. I suck in a breath when his fingers coast back and forth over my clit.

"Hmm, already so wet for me."

When aren't I? I swear I'm perpetually wet and ready for this man.

I spread my legs apart a little more to give him better access and allow my eyes to drift closed. He works his fingers back and forth and back and forth before one of them breaches my entrance. I suck in a breath and rock my hips, urging him to continue.

The vibrating of his phone interrupts my happy thoughts and Cole lets out a sigh and draws his hand away.

"To be continued," he says, dropping a kiss on the top of my head and rolling away from me to step out of bed. I watch him make his way across his bedroom to where his phone rests on his dresser, fascinated by the way the muscles in his perfect ass clench while he walks.

He lifts his phone up and looks at who's calling and a crease forms in the middle of his forehead. He hits the button to take the call.

"Hey, Steph. What's up?"

I now know that Steph is the blonde woman who bartends for him at the Thirsty Monk. The one woman who always gives me that predatory vibe where Cole is concerned.

He listens to her speak for a few seconds before responding.

"Calm down. I'm sure it's nothing. You're positive? Uh-huh. Okay. Hang tight. Don't worry. No, it's okay. I wasn't doing anything anyway."

His gaze snaps over to mine and I mask the sharp pain in my chest over his comment. She's obviously upset about something—maybe he's just trying to make her feel better.

"Yep. I'll be there as soon as I can." He hits end on the call and blows out a big breath before coming to sit beside me on the edge of the bed. "I have to go."

"Yeah, I gathered as much. Problem at the bar?" Maybe I'm asking to be conversational because it seems like the logical thing to say, but deep down I know I'm asking because I feel insecure. Which I hate.

"Not exactly."

Okay. I'll be honest. That answer doesn't instill much confidence in me.

"I shouldn't be too long. Why don't you stick around and I'll make dinner for us when I get back?"

"You don't mind me being in your place by myself?"

"Of course not."

That eases some of my lingering uneasiness.

He leans in and places a chaste kiss on my lips then rises from the bed to start getting dressed.

"I need to jump online and check out the job ads anyway. I'll take care of that while you're gone."

He nods as he lifts his jeans up to his hips, seeming a little preoccupied now. Another couple of minutes pass and he's fully dressed and walking over to me on the bed.

"I'll be back before you k now it." We kiss and moments later I hear the door to his place close and I'm left sitting in the middle of his big bed alone, feeling none of the warmth I usually do.

HOURS LATER I'VE SCOURED every online job site known to man, applied to a few that I'm more than qualified for, and I'm resting on the living room couch watching Sunday afternoon TV. Which is to say watching my third episode of *Storage Wars*. I stopped on this channel for a second just to check it out and somehow, I blink and it's three episodes later.

I hear something and I mute the TV. It sounds like a phone vibrating, so I hurry into Cole's bedroom thinking it's mine. I realize when I get there that it's Cole's phone ringing on the dresser. He must have forgotten it when he left in a rush. I don't pick it up, but I walk over to it and see the name Nadia flashing on the screen. Something about seeing the name of another woman on my . . . hell, I don't even know what to call him—my boyfriend, fuck buddy, friend with benefits? Whatever, something about seeing another woman's name on his phone lights a fire in the pit of my stomach.

I don't recognize the name and yes, she could be one of his employees whom I've never met, but something doesn't sit right in my gut about the whole situation. First Cole gets called out in the middle of the day by Steph for some reason he didn't seem too eager to divulge to me and now another woman I've never heard of is blowing up his phone.

The vibrating stops and a minute later a message appears on the screen, indicating that he has a new voice mail.

Before I can figure out how I want to handle this I hear the door to the condo open and Cole's heavy footsteps enter.

"Whit? You still here?"

I come walking out of the bedroom with what I'm hoping is a genuine-looking smile. "Right here."

"Sorry I was gone so long." His easy-going mood from earlier is gone and he seems tense and on edge. He has frown lines between his brows and the sparkle in his eyes has dimmed a fraction.

"Everything okay?"

"Yeah." He pulls me into him and wraps his arms around my body.

I lean into him and enjoy the cadence of his heartbeat in his chest, the soft feel of his shirt against my cheek. "Maybe I should go. You have your big meeting first thing in the morning. I don't want to be in the way."

He pulls away and looks down at me. "No. I want you to stay. Please?"

I study him for a moment. Something happened when he was gone. What I have no idea. But this isn't the same man who left six hours ago. "You sure?"

He nods and tucks a section of hair behind my ear. "Positive."

"Okay," I near-whisper.

I decide not to press him for answers and I'd like to say that it's because I'm confident he'll tell me when he's ready, but the reality is that a part of me doesn't want to know.

We've got a good thing going here and I'm not eager to mess it up. That makes sense, right?

I'M AWOKEN BY THE sound of my cell phone vibrating on the night stand beside me. At first, I moan and roll over, enjoying the vestiges of sleep too much to want to wake from my slumber.

But it begins vibrating again almost immediately. This time I crack my eyes open as much as they're able. The room is filled with a soft morning light. It's apparent that it's early, probably somewhere around dawn.

Who the hell would be calling me right now?

I reach out for my phone and tilt the screen toward me. It takes a moment for my eyes to focus. The sight of my grandparents' contact info sends a spike of fear straight through me. My pulse picks up immediately and I sit straight up in bed and slide my finger to answer.

"Hello?" Though my mind now feels alert, my voice hasn't caught up yet and still retains that raspy just-woken quality.

"Whitney? Oh, my dear." My grandma's voice sounds frightened and panicked and it dawns on me in the way that strange things do in a time of crisis that I've never heard her sound so afraid, even when Sparky chased the Jehovah's Witness who knocked on our door down the street.

"Grandma, what's wrong?"

"I'm on my way to the hospital. I had to call an ambulance." She breaks down and I picture her standing all alone in the middle of the kitchen, clutching the phone tight.

"Is everything okay?"

"I don't know. I don't know. Your grandpa got up in the middle of the night, I guess. I found him passed out in the hallway, blood pouring from his head."

My hand flies up to cover my mouth while she speaks and tears threaten to spill from my eyes.

"Are you still waiting for the ambulance?" I ask once I've removed my hand.

"They're just getting him in the ambulance now and we're headed to the emergency room."

"I'm coming, Grandma. You hang tight. I'll be there soon."

"Okay, dear. Okay."

I hit end on the call and spring from the bed.

"Hey." Cole's raspy voice comes from behind me while I attempt to locate my clothing. "What's going on?"

"My grandpa was taken to the hospital in an ambulance. I don't know much more than that, but I have to get there."

I pull my underwear up my legs and turn to face him. He's already out of bed and striding over to his dresser. "I'll drive you over."

"No, no, you don't have to come. You stay here. I can take an Uber or something." I bend down and pick my jeans up off the floor and shake them out so I can step into them.

"Whit, I'm not letting you take an Uber. No arguments."

I don't bother complaining because truth is I'm glad he's taking me. It'll be faster and having him near feels like a comfort—something I can use right now. Every conceivable scenario runs through my head. It's amazing how it only takes your brain a split second to conjure up a million terrible possibilities, but we can be so resistant to believe the good things.

When we're both dressed and I've managed to pull my dark bob back into the world's smallest ponytail, we race out of Cole's place, find where his Jeep is parked by the curb and speed off.

*chapter*

# TWENTY-NINE

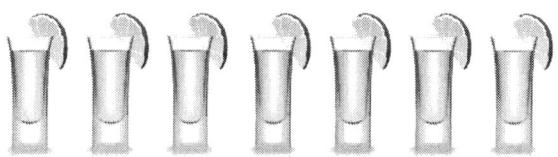

THE TWO OF US are silent on the drive over, though I can't manage to sit still. Eventually Cole reaches over and places a hand on my thigh and squeezes, a show of support that settles me somewhat.

It's all a blur, but we park and as soon as I run through the main doors to the emergency room I spot my grandma sitting in the uncomfortable-looking chairs in the waiting room, her arms wrapped around herself.

I slow my pace and walk over to her while the sterile scent of the hospital registers in my brain.

"Grandma." My voice breaks when I say her name.

She raises her head to look at me and then she stands. Wet stains are clear on her cheeks. We hug and I can tell that she's trying to hug me with all her might, but her frail body just doesn't have the strength it once did.

We pull away from one another but I keep my hands on her shoulders. "Have you heard anything from the doctors?" I ask.

She shakes her head. "No. No. Last I heard they're still running some tests."

"What happened?"

"I have no idea. Your grandpa wasn't feeling the best yesterday, but it didn't seem like anything serious."

I reach down and squeeze her hand in mine. "I'm sure he's going to be okay," I say, hoping it's the truth.

A single tear runs down her wrinkled cheek and she swipes it away. "I hope so. I don't know what I'd do without that big lug in my life." A sad smile forms on her face and her gaze flicks over my shoulder. "Oh, hi, Cole. I didn't see you there."

"Hi, Mrs. Knight. I'm sorry we're seeing each other under these circumstances."

"Enough with the Mrs. Knight stuff. Please call me Edna."

He pushes his hands into both his pockets and nods. "Can I get you ladies anything to drink? I'm going to run down to the cafeteria to grab a caffeine fix."

"I'd love a coffee," I say.

"I'm all right, thank you," my grandma says.

He nods. "Okay. I'll give you both a little privacy and be back in a bit." He leans in and kisses my forehead. I close my eyes for a second, thankful he's here.

"It seems the two of you are getting on okay," my grandma says while she takes a seat.

I sit in the chair beside her and reach over to take her hand in mine again. "Never mind that right now. Did the doctor or nurses give you any idea how long it would be before you got an update?"

She pats my hand and shakes her head. "They just said that they were going to do some tests to see what caused him to pass out. They were concerned about the fall and whether he hit his head hard enough to cause a concussion or something more serious." She presses her lips together and I get the sense that it's to try to stifle a cry.

"He's going to be okay, Grandma." I squeeze her hand.

"He's a tough guy."

"I sure hope so, sweetie. I sure hope so."

This time she does break out in tears and I wrap her in my arms and rock her back and forth, trying to comfort her, the same way she did with me when I was a child.

WHEN COLE RETURNS, I'M pacing back and forth in front of where my grandma sits. It feels like it's been eons that we've been out here waiting on some word and I can't stand to sit in that chair for another second.

"Here you go." He passes me a steaming cup of coffee. "Edna, I picked you up a bottle of water. I know you said you didn't want anything, but I figured you might change your mind."

He walks over to her and I can tell that she's moved by the small gesture.

"Thank you. That's very thoughtful of you." She pats his face and another small piece of my heart melts for him.

I sip my coffee and enjoy the way the hot liquid burns as it travels down my throat. It's a distraction from what we're doing here. It's not long before my mind wanders back to everything that's at stake though.

"How did you find him?" I ask my grandma.

"Sparky. That little thing wouldn't stop barking at me from the bottom of the bed, so I eventually got up thinking that maybe he wanted outside to go to the bathroom."

"Thank God he woke you." I've never loved that little mutt more than I do right now. That fur ball might be responsible for saving my grandpa's life.

My grandma nods, but her expression changes to panic.

"What's wrong?"

"I forgot all about Sparky. He's at the house and hasn't been fed or let out to go to the bathroom." Her shaky hand moves to her chest.

"I'll take care of it," Cole offers. We both turn in his direction. "That is, if you're comfortable with me going into your house without you there."

"It's not too much trouble, is it?" my grandma asks.

He shakes his head. "Not at all. In fact, why don't I keep him for a few days until you know what you're dealing with? It'll be one less thing for you to worry about."

"Oh, you're an angel. Thank you." She motions him over and when he gets near her she stands up and embraces him. "Thank you so much."

"Edna, I'm happy to help. You ladies have your hands full here."

A sad smile forms on my face. I'm so touched by his gesture, but I hate that we're here and it's necessary.

"Let me grab you my key." I walk over to the seat I left my purse on and dig through until I find my keychain. Once I have the house key pried off the thing I turn and place it in Cole's palm. "Let me walk you out," I say. "Grandma, I'll be right back."

She nods, preoccupied with her thoughts.

Cole slips the key into the front pocket of his jeans and takes my hand. Once we're outside by his Jeep he wraps me in a protective embrace.

"Try not to worry too much about your grandpa. I'm sure he's going to be fine." He kisses the top of my head and as silly as it is, his reassurance makes me feel a little better.

"I hope you're right."

"I am." He sounds so sure of himself. I wish I had his confidence.

"Thank you so much for dealing with Sparky. It's one less thing for—" I stop abruptly as I remember what day it is and my hands fly up to my face. "Oh, my God! Your big meeting was supposed to be this morning."

He takes my hands and pulls them away from my mouth. "I've already dealt with it. Don't worry."

My stomach flips. "What does that mean?"

"Relax." He places both hands on top of my shoulders. "I made a call and put off the meeting. We've rescheduled for next month."

"I feel terrible. I've ruined your big chance." My shoulders sag and he must feel it because he squeezes them both then bends down so we're eye level.

"You didn't ruin anything."

"How can you say that? This was your big shot."

"There'll be another big shot. Now don't worry about me. Worry about your grandparents, okay? Your grandma needs you right now."

I nod because he's right. I need to be strong right now so that I can support her through whatever it is that's going to happen.

"Okay." I'm not sure what to say—what combination of words will accurately express my level of gratitude right now. "I can't believe you did this, but thank you."

"Stop saying that, will you? You'd do the same for me."

He leans in and kisses me and I grip the front of his shirt tight because he's right. The depth of my feelings for him is disconcerting, but I don't think I'm in it alone. Otherwise, why would he be doing all of this?

When he pulls away he brushes a piece of hair off my face. "I'll go make sure Sparky is fed and take him for a walk then get him settled at my place. Then I'm going to head back here. Is there anything you need me to bring back with me?"

I shake my head. "Just you."

He smiles. "Promise. Now go take care of your grandma."

I turn and begin to walk away, then think better of it and look behind me to watch him pull away in his Jeep. I smile to myself even though there's not much to smile about at the moment.

AN HOUR LATER THE doctor comes out to tell us that my grandpa has walking pneumonia and that they think his fever caused him to pass out. He's suffered a concussion and they want to keep him in the hospital overnight, but they don't think there's any permanent damage to worry about.

I pull my phone out to text Cole the details as my grandma and I make our way through the maze of hallways in the hospital on the way to my grandpa's room.

Cole's texted me a couple of times to find out where Sparky's leash and food are. I couldn't help but laugh when he sent me a picture of Sparky trying to hump his leg as soon as he got in the door.

I finish up the text as we reach the room and slip my phone into my purse.

My grandma leads the way and I follow in behind her to see my grandpa sitting in bed with a large bandage covering his head. Apparently, he needed quite a few stitches to close the gash he received. His eyes are closed and his pallor is a little gray, but beyond that he looks to be okay.

"Seems like he's resting," my grandma says to me.

Not for long. My grandpa's eyes flutter open and he gives a weak smile. "Edna, you're here."

My grandma wastes no time in moving one of the chairs in the room over to his bedside. I follow suit and pull one up on the other side while the two of them embrace.

"You almost scared us to death," I fake-scold.

My grandpa pats my hand in a gentle gesture. He's putting on a brave face, but I can tell that he's weak.

"Nothing a little medicine won't cure."

"How are you feeling?" my grandma asks.

"Don't you two lovely ladies worry about me. I've got a lot of life left in me yet."

"For real though, Grandpa. How are you?" I pin him with a stare that lets him know I'm not going to back down until I get a straight answer.

"I'm a little woozy and my head is pounding from that fall. This fever has me feeling like crap, but whatever they've given me seems to be helping a bit with that."

I grip my grandpa's hand in both of mine. "I'm so relieved that you're okay."

"Me, too," my grandma echoes. "I don't know what I'd ever do without you, Lawrence."

He shakes his head in annoyance. "You two need to stop carrying on. I'm fine."

"You're not fine. You could have been killed if you'd passed out on the stairs or if you'd lain there bleeding for too long. Next time you don't feel well, Lawrence, you'd better bet that I'm dragging you to the doctor's office."

My grandpa simply shakes his head and rolls his eyes, knowing better than to argue with my grandma when she means business.

My phone buzzes in my purse so I pull it out and see that Cole's made it to his house with Sparky. He's sent a picture of the little mutt in his bed—on the side that I normally sleep on—with the caption, *Looks like someone is gunning for your spot.*

I laugh a little.

"What's so funny, hun?" my grandma asks.

"Oh nothing. Cole was just letting me know that he and Sparky have made it to his place."

"He's a keeper, that one," my grandma says and then winks at me. She's fussing with the blankets on the hospital bed while my grandpa tries to get her to stop. "What exactly is going on with you two?"

"I wish I knew," I reply honestly.

My grandpa gives up on trying to get my grandma to stop fussing with him and leans his head back against his pillow and closes his eyes.

"You two will figure it out," she says. "I've seen the way he looks at you."

I slipped my phone back into my purse. "How's that?"

Her gaze slides over to my grandpa and a reverent smile forms on her lips. "The same way your grandpa looked at me when he was falling in love."

My face grows hot.

I'm not sure what to say, but I don't want to let her know how happy her words make me. I don't dare hope that she's right.

# chapter
# THIRTY

*I*'VE BARELY SEEN COLE over the past week—I've been so preoccupied with nursing my grandpa back to health and making sure my grandma isn't overdoing it.

Now that he's on the mend my thoughts have fallen back to my job search and Cole. Tonight, my focus is Cole though, because who finds a job on a Friday night?

He had plans to go out with his brother, but even so . . . when Lennon called to see if I wanted to go out with her and Tahlia, I made up an excuse. I want to be waiting for Cole when he returns home tonight.

He's given me a key to use when I'm supposed to meet him at his place and I figure tonight is as good a time as any to put it to use.

*Me: What time do you think you'll be home?*

*Cole: Not too late. Probably around midnight . . .*

*Me: Mind if I wait for you at your place? I have a surprise for you.*

*Cole: Do tell.* ☺

*Me: No way. You can unwrap it when I see you. ;)*

Halloween is in a few days and I picked up a slutty devil costume to surprise him. I want to thank him for how supportive he's been about the situation with my grandpa. Sparky is settled back home and life is beginning to return to normal. I can't afford a weekend getaway or anything like that, but when I passed by a lingerie store the other day while out picking up my grandpa's prescription, I had the idea that Cole might enjoy something better anyway.

*I know I would.*

I use Cole's key when I arrive at his place and let myself in. It's only around eleven, but I want to make sure I'm there with plenty of time to change and get ready.

By eleven thirty I'm decked out in red thigh-high stockings, a lace and latex bustier with matching G-string and heels. A headband with little devil's ears completes my get-up. The bright red color sets off my pale skin and dark hair nicely, if I do say so myself.

I position myself on his couch at the perfect angle to showcase all the goodies and wait.

And wait.

And wait.

Finally, at one a.m. I pull my phone out to see if he's texted me. Nothing.

Should I see where he's at? He's off enjoying a boys' night with his brother and whoever else. I'm sure they're probably just having a good time and maybe he lost track of time.

I decide to send him a text that isn't demanding, but might serve as a gentle reminder that I'm still here waiting.

*Me: Can't wait for you to unwrap your surprise! ;)*

It's close to two a.m. before I doze off and he still hasn't returned or even viewed my text.

I awake to a pair of large hands running up and down over my ass and dipping between my thighs. My cheek is pressed into the fabric of the couch and it takes me a moment to get my bearings before I realize where I am.

"Mmm, I really like my surprise." Cole's voice heats my blood instantly and I shake off the last vestiges of sleep.

"What time is it?" I ask.

Either he ignores my question or he didn't hear it. "Sorry I got hung up." He squeezes both of my ass cheeks and lets out a sound that's a mix between a moan and a growl. My nipples tighten behind the red lace in response.

I'm still lying on my tummy while Cole's hands explore my body and I take a quick glance over at the cable box to see that it's a little past five a.m.

"Is everything okay?" I ask.

"It is now." He leans forward and kisses the spot where my neck meets my shoulder and I close my eyes, letting my head fall to the side to give him better access.

I can smell the alcohol on him. He and his friends must have had a good time tonight.

With no warning, Cole lifts me by the waist and moves me forward so that I'm hanging over the arm of the couch, my elbows resting on the end table.

I yelp, but then wiggle my hips as his fingers slide the G-string down my legs, past my heels before he uses his hands to spread me. I'm bared for him to see.

"Your pussy is as pretty as the rest of you."

I wonder for a second why he wouldn't have let me know he was going to be so late, or why he didn't return my text.

I don't voice my concern though. Partly because I'm not sure I really want to know the answer and partly because at that moment Cole's tongue is running up the length of my pussy. He dips it into my entrance.

How am I supposed to think clearly when he's doing that?

He pulls back for a second. "I hope you're in the mood for rough, sweetheart."

I nod my agreement, unable to form any words. Right now, I'm in the mood for whatever he's willing to give me. Every nerve in my body is firing off as his tongue laps at me.

He concentrates his efforts on my clit, pulling and licking, and then pushes two fingers inside me, scissoring them so that he's stretching me in the most delicious way. I push back on his fingers, so close to coming.

Cole removes his mouth from me and straightens out on his knees behind me. I assume he's about to fuck me but instead he uses one hand to circle over my mound and the other fucks me with his fingers at a rapid pace. There's no chance for me to catch my breath and the intensity catches me off guard. I'm like a stick of dynamite with the match just out of reach. When he slaps my clit with his hand I buck back against him and cry out as the match lights the fuse and I explode. I'm lost in a sea of ecstasy and I don't want anyone to throw me a life raft because this feels too damn exquisite.

He slows his movements and brings me down from my orgasm, eventually pulling away from me. The couch cushion shifts and I know he's now standing beside it.

"What did you boys get into tonight?" I pant and fall back onto my heels so I can turn and face him. "You're a wild man." My comment is meant to be playful, but I can see instantly that I've touched on something.

His gaze is as intense as it's ever been and his hands clench at his sides. Cole's usual calm demeanor is absent and now there's a storm raging inside him, yet I have no idea why.

"What's wrong?" I ask.

"I need you. That's all."

He pulls me up and into his chest so that my soft meets his hard and his lips find mine in a savage fury. His tongue pushes into my mouth and I match his intensity. He's ready to devour me and I'm absolutely ready to let him. It's almost addictive being wanted by this man.

Cole's lips trail a path down my neck, igniting a fire in my veins.

"I need you so bad right now, my little devil," he murmurs into my skin. He roughly grabs at my breast through the lace and though I get the sense that he's using me to push something else away, I don't care.

This man has become the center of my universe and I'll happily give him anything he needs.

He kisses my collarbone and then reaches for the lace that covers my breasts. He pulls the fabric down so that my tits are bared, but my mid-section is still covered by the latex portion of the bustier.

Cole stares hungrily at my chest and grips one breast in each of his hands, sliding his thumbs back and forth over my nipples—nipples that are growing harder and more sensitive by the second.

"Your tits are so perfect. I can't believe I still haven't fucked these yet."

"No time like the present." And suddenly that's all I want. For him to push me to my knees, squeeze my tits together, and thrust that perfect, unicorn cock of his between them while I watch him come undone.

And so I do just that. I lower myself to my knees, but then there's a loud banging on the door.

"Cole! We need to talk!"

I recognize the voice as Chase's and wonder what the hell he's doing here this early in the morning.

"Shit." Cole quickly helps me to my feet. "Go hide in the bedroom until I can get rid of him."

I'm still standing here stunned at the quick turn of events when he walks over to the door.

Chase bangs again. "Open up! I know you're there! Quit fucking around!"

Cole looks over his shoulder at me. "Go!" he whisper-shouts.

I move into action, scurrying into the bedroom and closing the door. Once I'm in there I put my regular clothes back on as fast as possible in case I am discovered. The only thing worse than that would be if it happened while I'm wearing slutty devil lingerie.

I hear Cole open the door and greet his brother. And okay, maybe I have my ear pressed up against the door, but so what? This place was built more than a century ago and has thin walls and poor insulation so it's not like I couldn't hear their conversation even if I wasn't trying so hard. I want to know what has Chase worked up into such a tizzy. Maybe Neiman Marcus ran out of his favorite pair of designer dress socks.

I cover my mouth and stifle a laugh at the thought.

"This isn't a good time." I can hear the bite in Cole's tone. What has him so annoyed with his brother?

"I don't give a shit. You'd better make time or Dad's going to find out about your little secret."

*What the hell does that mean?*

Cole mumbles something that I can't catch.

"Why the fuck did you take off like that? The party was just starting to get good," Chase says.

"I told you before that I want no part in that. You need to come clean."

"And let a few pieces of ass ruin the future I have so carefully planned out? Forget it."

I gasp and cover my mouth with my hand.

"Maybe you should have thought of that before," Cole says, sounding more than a little pissed.

"Come on, man. You know how it is." Chase must have moved because he sounds closer to me now. "It's just for fun. Those girls don't mean anything. I love Tahlia, but the thought of fucking the same girl for eternity doesn't exactly sound like heaven."

*Oh, God. Poor Tahlia.*

I wrap my arms around my middle and press my ear against the door harder, not wanting to miss anything.

"I don't know what you want me to say."

"I want you to tell me you'll continue to keep my secret and stay out of my business."

"She's going to find out. You know that, right?"

I hear footsteps on the hardwood floor. "Not if you keep your mouth shut."

"Get your hands off me. I don't even know how you can live with yourself," Cole says.

"Don't give me that holier-than-thou bullshit." Chase's voice is louder now and has an angrier edge. "You used to fuck a new woman every night. I think you've probably fucked half the girls who work for you." Chase laughs and I try hard to push away the memories of Cole deep in conversation with Steph from the Thirsty Monk. "You think any of those broads knew they wouldn't be sticking around? You think they knew they'd be nothing more than a Webber wench?"

I press my lips together and my eyes widen.

"What the fuck did you just say?" Cole asks in a low voice fuelled with venom.

Chase laughs but it's bitter-sounding. "That's what Tahlia and all her friends call all the girls you bang. Webber wenches. Seems appropriate."

There's some silence first and then some grunting and

finally a bang on the bedroom door. I jump back, my heart racing.

"I've told you that you need to come clean. I'm sick of this shit. Either you tell her or I will."

I think Cole must have Chase pressed up against the door.

"Fuck you. You've got your own secrets, bro. And if you don't keep your mouth shut Dad's going to find out about all the women."

Cole must let Chase go because I hear him stomp off and then the door to Cole's place slams shut a few seconds later.

That's when it really hits me. This isn't a surprise to Cole. He knew. He *knew* Chase was cheating on Tahlia and he didn't say anything. He lied to me. For how long I don't know.

Bile burns the back of my throat. I suck in a breath and will myself not to cry, though my eyes burn with unshed tears and I realize I'm shaking.

When I push the bedroom door open Cole stands with his back to me, his head hung low. He pushes a hand through his hair and turns to face me.

Defeat is all over his face. Everything that I just heard settles on my chest and it feels as if my lungs are shrinking, leaving me with no air to breathe.

My best friend's fiancé is cheating on her and I have to be the one to tell her. I squeeze my eyes shut for a second, knowing how much pain I'm going to cause her. The man she's in love with has been lying to her for who knows how long. And, it seems, so too has the man I love.

"Whit, let me explain." He takes a couple of steps toward me, but I put my hand up to stop him. I don't want him anywhere near me.

"How long have you known?" It's ironic because the voice that leaves my mouth is dead and void of all the emotion that feels like it's slowly suffocating me.

"It's not what you think."

"How. Long?" My jaw begins to ache from how hard I'm clenching my teeth together.

"A month or so."

"I am such an idiot." I pass him and rush to the living room where my bag is. Thank God Chase didn't notice it. Once I snatch it up I turn to leave but Cole's already standing in front of the door blocking my exit.

"Where are you going?" There's a desperate edge to his voice.

"Where do you think I'm going? I'm off to break my friend's heart!" I yell. I want to scream and rage at him for breaking mine, too, but I can't think about that right now.

Tahlia is engaged to Chase. They're supposed to be getting married in the spring. My problem is miniscule compared to hers right now.

"We have to talk," he pleads and the expression on his face almost makes me want to hear whatever pathetic excuse he has for not being honest with me, but I don't feed into it. What would be the point? More lies? More untruths?

I know better than to think someone won't let me down. I let myself get swept up in Cole, but this is the reminder I needed.

"Please just get away from the door." I'm staring down at the ground by his feet. I can't even bear to look at him.

"Whit, you can't do this. Please. Not like this."

I return my gaze to his. "I can't believe you have the balls to say that to me after you've been lying to me for so long. Move."

With a long sigh his shoulders slump and he steps to the side to let me pass.

I don't glance in his direction as my shaking hand grips the door handle and turns. Before I can open it, his hand grips my arm above my elbow.

God, I hate that the feel of his hand on my arm still has the ability to make my skin sing. How pathetic am I?

I look over at him and I'm met with such anguish in his hazel eyes that my breath catches. "This isn't over."

A lone tear trails down my cheek and my bottom lip trembles for a second before I manage to swallow past the painful lump in my throat. "It was over before it even began. I just didn't know it."

He drops his hand and I pull the door open and march out into the hall, leaving my shattered heart at his doorstep.

# chapter
# THIRTY-ONE

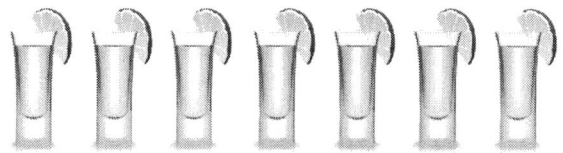

A S SOON AS I exit Cole's house I call up Lennon, not caring about the time, and fill her in on everything that's happened.

"That motherfucker," she says. "I'm going to rip his balls off and feed them to him myself."

"Agreed." I'm walking as fast as I can away from Cole's place, in no particular direction. Anything to put some space between us. "We need to go over to Tahl's right now and tell her what's been going on."

Lennon takes a big sigh. "Okay, where are you? I'll pick you up on the way over."

I glance around the residential street I've ended up on. "I'm not even sure. I'll text you a crossroads when I end up somewhere I know."

"Sounds good. Give me a few to get dressed and then I'm leaving."

"Okay."

"Whit . . . how are you doing with all this?" The sympathy in her voice has me sucking back a sob.

"Let's not worry about me. Right now, I'm concerned with how Tahlia's going to handle this."

She's quiet for a moment and knowing her like I do there's something she wants to say, but in a rare show of restraint she refrains, instead just saying, "I'll see you soon," and hangs up.

Everything in me wants to break down and rage and fall apart over Cole's betrayal, but there will be plenty of time for that after I destroy my best friend with what I know.

TAHLIA SITS AND STARES ahead at me, appearing almost catatonic in her response to everything I just told her. Once I began it all just came spewing out and she knows everything now. About hooking up with Cole before I knew it was him, about carrying on with Cole *after* I knew it was him, and about Chase—her cheating bastard of a fiancé.

We're in Tahlia's living room and Lennon and I keep glancing from each other back to Tahl waiting for her to say something.

To react.

Anything.

After at least two minutes of silence I can't take it any longer. "Tahl? Say something."

She blinks a couple of times and turns her head in my direction. "You're sure? There's no chance this is some kind of mistake or misunderstanding?" Her voice cracks a couple of times.

I shake my head. "No. I heard it all myself."

"Because you were at Cole's place . . . because you two are . . ."

My shoulders sag, the guilt from keeping her in the dark weighing on me. "I didn't plan it. You have to believe me. You know how I felt about him before all of this. He's the last person I would have guessed I'd share a connection with."

"I told her not to tell you at first." Lennon raises her hand as if she's in fifth-grade math class and the way the corner of her lips tug down tells me that she's second-guessing that decision like I am. "We just thought you had enough going on and one more thing to worry about wouldn't be helpful."

"I didn't think it would amount to anything," I admit, looking down to my lap. The piercing feeling in my chest betrays my expectations.

"Do you . . . love him?" Tahlia asks in a small voice.

"I don't want to," I admit.

She nods her head as if she understands that sentiment completely, and right now she probably does.

"Do you forgive me?" I ask.

"And me?" Lennon adds.

She looks from me to Lennon and back. "Guys, of course I do. I understand. I really do. I have been so stressed out lately and you're right. I don't know how I would have reacted."

Though I still feel badly, a little of the guilt that's been weighing me down eases.

"You're worrying me, Tahl. I expected tears and maybe you throwing a few things."

"I just . . . I'm in shock, I think." She stands and grabs her purse off her kitchen counter and heads toward the front door.

"Where are you going?" I ask, tailing behind her.

"I need to see Chase." She seems eerily calm and collected for what I've just told her. I'm more than a little concerned.

"You're still in your pyjamas," I say.

She looks down at herself for a second and then shrugs absentmindedly.

"Do you want us to go with you?" Lennon asks.

She shakes her head. "No. This is something I need to do myself."

"Let me drive you over there," Lennon offers.

"Yeah, Tahl." I reach out and still the hand that's reaching down for her shoe. "You don't have to do this alone."

She looks from me to Lennon and back, tears now dotting the corner of her eyes. "I do though. Thank you for telling me. Not everyone would."

I've never had a thank you make me feel worse than this one.

"Call us as soon as you leave his place," Lennon says.

"We'll wait here for you."

She nods, her eyes vacant, and turns and leaves. Lennon and I are left alone in her place, neither one of us speaking because really, there are no words that are going to make anyone feel better right now.

There is, however, wine. I walk back into the kitchen to check out Tahlia's wine fridge.

Who cares if it's only eight in morning?

⟲⟳

I SET MY PEN down on the page I'm writing on and close my journal when there's a knock on my bedroom door.

"Come in." The depression in my voice rings clear, but I'm unconcerned.

There was no hiding my absolute devastation when I returned home from Tahlia's a few days ago. Or my drunkenness. When my grandma pressed me to know why I was intoxicated by dinnertime I'd broken down in her arms and confessed to her all that had happened.

My grandma pokes her head through my door but doesn't enter. "Hi, sweetheart." The term of endearment causes a stabbing pain in my chest because that's what Cole used to call me.

"Hey," I manage to croak out.

"Cole is here. He wants to talk to you."

I sit up ramrod straight on my mattress. "What is he doing here?"

I know the answer so I'm not sure why I ask. He's grown desperate. I wouldn't take any of the hundred calls he's made to me or return his texts. In fact, I went so far as to block him entirely so that I wouldn't have to see his name light up my phone screen anymore.

"He said he needs to explain everything to you."

"Pfft. He can shove his explanation up his—" My grandma looks her nose down at me and I press my lips together. "Sorry. He can shove it where the sun don't shine."

My grandma steps into the room and closes the door softly behind her, then takes a seat beside me on the bed.

"You know, hearing him out might help you feel better. Let you move on."

"I'm already moving on." *Lie.* "I hardly miss him at all." *Bigger lie.* "I have no desire to see him at all." *I wish that was true.*

My grandma wraps an arm around my shoulders. "Are you sure? He looks really torn up."

This brings me an immense amount of pleasure. I'm glad to know he's hurting, too. He deserves to.

"Are you defending him?" I pull away from her embrace and stand from my bed.

"Of course not. What he did was wrong. But people do some stupid things when they're scared, Whitney. Maybe you should hear him out." The expression on her face is pleading but she's not going to sway me.

I've already proven that I'm weak by getting involved with him in the first place. Why don't I ever learn? My experience with my boss should have taught me what happens when I mess with someone I know I shouldn't be involved with.

Pain.

Devastation.

Heartbreak.

I'm an idiot for signing up for all of that for a second time.

I thought Cole was different . . . for a second I thought that maybe he could be . . . the one.

*I'm such an idiot.*

I cross my arms over my chest. "You can tell Cole to go away and not to bother coming back. I won't be talking to him—not today, not ever."

She frowns and stands from the bed. "If that's what you really want."

"It is."

She leaves without another word and closes the door behind her.

Once I hear her making her way down the staircase I collapse onto my bed and fall apart.

We started as enemies, became lovers, and are back to being enemies again.

Funny, I always thought full-circle moments were supposed to be a *good* thing.

# chapter
# THIRTY-TWO

*I* SETTLE INTO THE chair in Mr. Jeffries' office and instead of being insanely nervous like the first time I was here, I'm more curious than anything. I have no clue why I was called here today, but at this point if he were to offer me the job of cleaning gum off his shoes I'd take it if the pay was decent.

My last couple of weeks have been spent at rock bottom and I'm tired of the view. I'm willing to take any minuscule improvement in my situation.

I hear footsteps and turn to see him wander in with a smile on his face, not looking as if he's in too much of a hurry even though I've been waiting in here for more than five minutes.

"Whitney! I'm so sorry to keep you waiting."

"It's no trouble." *Not like I have anywhere else to be,* I think to myself.

I rise from my chair to shake his hand before he takes a seat at his desk. I sit back down and perch myself on the end of the chair, anxious to know what this impromptu meeting is about. Did they find out about that extra mint I took from the basket in reception the last time I was here?

"I'm sure you're wondering why I asked you to stop by today." I nod and bite the inside of my cheek to keep from blurting out that I just want him to get on with it. "As you know when we originally filled the position you'd interviewed for we decided to go in a different direction."

God, I hate that term. Just say it for what it is—you thought someone was better than me. Not like I'm not used to it.

"That decision proved to be a mistake. You're here today because I'd like to offer you the position you originally interviewed for. If you're still interested?"

My adrenaline spikes and my entire body hums. Did he just say what I think he did?

"Are you still interested?" he asks because I'm still sitting here like I lack the brain cells to form an intelligent response.

"Yes. Yes! Yes!" I sound like some chick in a rom-com movie accepting a proposal.

I spring up from my seat and before I can stop myself I'm around to the other side of his desk hugging him. "Yes! I'm so excited. I'm going to do the best job. I'm going to be the best damn investigative reporter you've ever seen!"

I pull away. His eyes are wide and he appears slightly panicked at my reaction.

I cower down, back stepping away from him. "I'm so sorry. That was completely unprofessional of me."

He leans back in his seat and smooths his now crumpled tie down his chest. Oh, my God. I basically just dry-humped my new boss. My new *gay* boss. He probably didn't even enjoy it.

"Here, let me." I reach forward and smooth his tie for him for a few seconds before it dawns on me that this too is totally inappropriate. I raise my hands up and round the desk to my designated side.

"I'm just going to stop touching you now, okay?"

He chuckles and gestures to the chair on the other side of

his desk so I reclaim my seat. "I like your enthusiasm, Whitney. I do. But let's just keep our hands to ourselves, shall we?"

"'Can't keep my hands to myself,'" I sing in the same melody as Selena Gomez's song. I pinch the bridge of my nose.

*Oh, my God, Whitney, shut up before you ruin this.*

"Of course," I finally manage.

"All right then. I'm going to send you down to human resources. They already have a contract drafted up for you to review and sign so you can start right away. The original person who had the job had to leave suddenly."

"May I ask why it didn't work out with her? It might help me to do my own job better if I know what you don't like."

My boss straightens some papers on his desk before answering. "Well, if you don't go on a bender every night and show up to work high as a kite, we should be good."

I bite my bottom lip and nod. "I think I can handle that. Contrary to what you might think based on my reaction here today, I'm not actually on drugs."

"Glad to hear it."

I hear someone walk by the office and Mr. Jeffries' gaze flickers to the door for a second. "Kelsey."

The footsteps stop and back track. A second later the girl I met while I was interviewing pokes her head in the door.

"Kelsey, Whitney here is going to be starting with us immediately. Think you can do me a favor and show her to human resources? They're expecting her."

She looks over at me, and smiles. "Of course."

I rise from my chair and lean across the desk to shake my new boss' hand. "Thank you so much for this opportunity. I promise I won't disappoint you."

"I believe it. Welcome to WHFI."

A genuine smile spreads across my face. It feels foreign because I haven't smiled like this since . . . besides with Cole, I can't remember when.

Kelsey waits until we're out of earshot of Mr. Jeffries' office before she does a little squeal and grips my arm. "I'm so excited that we're going to be working together!"

"So am I!" I say in a low voice. "I've been tuning in and you're doing a great job."

She smiles and squeezes my arm. "Thank you. I think you're really going to like it here. For the most part everyone is pretty cool."

"I need this in my life more than you can possibly understand. So, what happened with the other girl?"

"Treena? She was on the hot mess express, believe me."

I nod. "How was everyone when you came on board?"

She slows her steps a bit and I follow suit. "I think a few people might have had a problem with it. They weren't outwardly rude, but they weren't exactly welcoming either, if you know what I mean. Now that some time has passed and they see that I'm not as dumb as I look"—she does a quick gesture to her blonde locks and her large chest—"they're much better. Most people don't like change and I don't think they were keen on having a young girl get the job, especially for the sportscaster position."

"Okay. Good to know." Nervous energy seeps in, replacing the earlier adrenaline that was coursing through my system.

We reach the other side of the building a couple of seconds later and Kelsey points to one of the offices. "That's where you need to be. When you're done come find me and maybe we can grab lunch together."

"That'd be great," I say, meaning it.

Maybe things are finally turning around for me.

I nix that thought as soon as it enters my head. That kind of thinking never seems to work out well for me.

*chapter*

# THIRTY-THREE

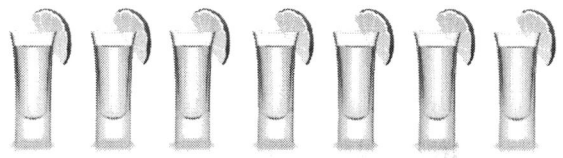

L ENNON TRIES TO FIX my hair for the third time since she showed up at my house to pick me up. "Will you stop? What gives?"

"I want you to look perfect." She tugs my shirt down a bit so that I'm showing more cleavage.

"Why? We're just going out for drinks. What's the big deal?"

"No big deal. None," she says as she turns the key and starts her old van, then pulls her seat belt across her chest and secures it.

I study her for a second and she's fidgeting, which means . . . she's lying. "Lennon, what's going on?"

"What do you mean?" she asks in her put-on innocent voice that I know better than to believe.

"Why do you seem like you're hiding something?" I shift in my seat so I'm facing her.

She shrugs, but doesn't say anything and then takes a right at the corner.

"Why are you going this way?" I ask. "I thought we were going to go to our usual place."

We now frequent the pub where Lennon picked up the

bartender. Apparently, she likes the atmosphere and since he's not a clinger she's okay hanging out there. If the mood strikes her she takes him home.

I may not be speaking to my bartender, but she's still speaking to hers. Sadness tries to creep into my chest, but I push it back.

I can't go there. The thought of Cole brings tears to my eyes almost every time and I'm determined to have fun tonight. And that means no thinking about what I lost.

"I'm taking a different route. There's construction going on everywhere these days."

"Uh-huh." I lean back into my seat and cross my arms over my chest. She's up to *something*. Of that I'm certain. I suppose I'll have to keep my guard up and see what it is. If she's not trying to set me up with anyone it should be fine.

As her unicorn van weaves its way through the city streets I gaze out the window, happy to sit in silence while the scenery passes me by. My mind wanders back to Cole, like it always does, and the heavy weight of disappointment and loss perches itself on my shoulders. The weight is now so much a part of me that it feels like something is missing in those rare moments it's not present.

I become cognizant of our whereabouts when Lennon pulls the vehicle into the parking lot of Rock Hard Whiskey and I whip my head around in her direction. "What the hell are we doing here?"

She presses her lips together, but says nothing as she finds an empty spot and parks. I realize that the parking lot is packed. Who do all these cars belong to?

Panic flares up inside and I try to slow my breathing but it feels like there's a heavy brick lying on my chest.

Lennon removes the keys and tosses them into her purse. I can't believe I was so dense. Looking at what she's wearing, I know it should've been more obvious to me that she had a plan in place. Gone is the graphic tee and jeans she's normally wearing and in place of it is a pair of black cigarette pants and a fancier cream tank with black leather jacket over the top. Jeez, am I blind or what?

"So . . . before you lose your shit on me let me just say something. You need closure. Regardless of how things turn out between you and Cole you need to talk to him, let him explain himself and figure it out from there."

Feeling defensive, I cross my arms over my chest. "What I need is to get away from here."

"Whit, you didn't get to say anything to Cole when he stood you up at that restaurant all those years ago, and look where that got you. You were wrong about the kind of person he was and you ended up falling in love with him. What are the chances there's more than meets the eye here now?"

She waits patiently while I mull that over. Lennon isn't saying anything that hasn't already crossed my mind in the weeks since our big blowout. Still . . . I haven't wanted to go there because being hurt once was enough, thank you very much. I'm not going to willingly set myself up again. Which is why every time Cole called or showed up at my grandparents' house, I refused to see him. Nothing can change the fact that he knowingly lied to me.

"And if I talk to him we can leave?"

She reaches forward and squeezes my arm. "Yes! You hear him out and if afterwards you want to go get plastered at the bar, I'm game. I'll even hold your hair back from your face while you're puking." She winks.

I draw in a deep breath. It's gut check time.

I suppose I knew this would all come to a head at some point, but now that it's here my flight response is kicking in hard. I chew on my bottom lip for a second and tell myself it's all going to be okay. I'm a big girl and I've dealt with worse. I'll get through this. I can do this.

I don't speak as I open the door and step out of the van. Lennon walks beside me as we head toward the building, a silent pillar of support. A low beat of music comes from inside the building.

"What's going on here tonight?" I ask.

"I'll let Cole explain."

It's like a tiny fist reaches into my chest and squeezes my heart when I hear her statement. Not because I'm jealous, but because I'm supposed to be the one who knows what's going on in Cole's life. I should be the one he's telling—not her.

"Wait." My hand stills on the door handle. "What about Tahl? Does she know about this?" I can't help but feel like a traitor by cracking the door open even a little and allowing Cole the opportunity to explain. What if he wedges his foot in and before I know it the door blows wide open?

"She knows we're here and she wants you to be happy. If that means being with Cole she's fine with it, so long as she doesn't have to see Chase. Obviously."

I nod and pull open the door, sucking in another deep breath to calm my nerves.

It's clear there's some type of event being held here tonight. The sound of music and the murmur of a crowd echo out of the door leading to the main part of the distillery. I lead us past the reception area, through the doorway, and straight into the middle of a party in full swing.

Not only is there a party here where there was once an empty warehouse, but the entire ambiance of the space has changed. Strings of clear lights have been hung way up on the ceiling in a criss-cross pattern, giving a warm glow over the space. People are seated at the round tables that dot the room and others stand on what I'm assuming must be the dance floor. A sound system has been set up discreetly along the perimeter of the space and the decor on the tables matches the feel of the many whiskey barrels stacked along the back wall—sort of a country chic.

I remember back to when we were checking out venues for Tahlia and Chase and how Cole had a million questions for the woman at the Bluxome Street Winery. It all makes sense now.

"Let's grab a drink." Lennon motions over to a bar that's been set up on the far side of the room.

I follow her and we weave our way through the crowd, none of whom I recognize, though. I think I might have spotted Ashley and Brady over in the far corner. No sign of Cole yet. My pulse thrums in my ears as I stand in line at the bar waiting to order a drink, waiting to see Cole again for the first time in weeks, waiting to hear what he has to say. All of it this time around.

I feel him before I smell him.

I smell him before I hear him.

I hear him before I see him.

"Ladies, glad to see you here." His deep timbre rings out from behind me like it's in a vacuum. He's all I hear. The constant murmur of the crowd around me and the baseline of the music evaporate into nothing. I brace myself as I turn in his direction.

One thing I've realized through all of this is that just because someone hurt you doesn't mean that you get to stop loving them. On the contrary, it only hurts because you *do* still love them so much. Love isn't a switch that you can turn on and off at will, which is why as Cole stands there feasting his gaze upon me in a fitted charcoal suit with white dress shirt open at the collar, my heart flips in my chest. Because the sight of him still draws a reaction from my body even though I swore I never wanted to see him again.

My breath hitches and my voice locks.

"Whit, you look devastating." He leans in and places a kiss on my cheek. It's quick, but it has its intended effect—both reminding me of and leaving me longing for the days when being close to him was a given. "Lennon, thank you for bringing her."

"Well, you're on your own now. My work here is done." She turns and reaches for the drink the bartender just placed down in front of her. "I'm off to mingle like I'm single. Which I am." She shrugs. "Whit, come find me when you want to go."

"Okay," I say, my eyes unwavering from Cole's.

Then she turns to address Cole, her expression as hard as steel. "If one of you Webber boys hurts my friends again I'll strap you down and tattoo the fuck out of your testicles. Got it?" She raises a brow at Cole. His jaw twitches, but he nods. "Good boy." She pats his chest and then disappears into the crowd.

His attention lands back on me and I shift my weight onto my heels. "She's a good friend."

"The best," I agree.

"When I called her she made me jump through a bunch of hoops before she agreed to try to get you here tonight."

"Good." I cross my arms in front of me, causing my cleavage to push up out of the low-cut V shirt that Lennon forced me to wear tonight. Cole's gaze dips to it for a second and my nipples pebble.

Jeez, didn't my nips get the memo? We are *not* having sex with this man again.

"Can we go somewhere more quiet to talk?"

I know quiet must mean alone and alone is not good. Alone means there's the possibility of the two of us being tempted to be physical and right now I feel like a starving woman at the world's largest buffet and Cole is the mile-long tray of éclairs, cakes and ice cream.

"Let's talk here. Say what you have to say so that I can leave."

"Sweetheart . . ." He reaches forward and cups my cheek and that's all it takes. One face-cupping and I'm putty in his hands.

"Fine. Let's get this over with." I lean away from his touch.

This is already hard enough.

He clenches his jaw, but he doesn't say anything, instead motioning for me to follow him. Which I do. He leads me to a door in the back corner of the room where he holds it open and lets me walk through. It opens to a tall set of stairs that must go up to the roof.

"Are you planning to throw me off the roof?" I deadpan as I take the first few steps up.

"Hardly. I'm taking my own life in your hands by leading you up there," he says, following me. "I just figure this is the only place we can get away from the music and have some privacy."

I reach the top of the long flight of stairs and push the door open. We are indeed on the flat roof of the building and not too far ahead of me is a fur blanket that has been laid out with a few more blankets tossed to the side of that one. Surrounding those are a handful of candles in glass mason jars. It's a full moon so I'm able to make out quite a bit, even without the added light. The entire set-up screams romance and I turn to give Cole a questioning gaze.

"This seemed like a really good idea when it was in my head, but looking at it now I can see how you might have the wrong idea." He looks flustered and he walks forward, blowing out a couple of the candles before I stop him.

"It's fine, Cole. Just leave them."

He turns to face me and wrings a hand through his hair. "I swear I don't plan on seducing you. I just wanted you to be warm and comfortable. All I want is to explain everything."

I nod and shiver a bit, images of Cole's seduction coming to mind. He mistakes the action for me being cold.

"Come have a seat. Use a blanket to warm up." He bends over and picks up one of the beige fur blankets and holds it out for me to take.

It's late fall, but the weather tonight is mild. Chances are it's probably in the low to mid-fifties, but I don't argue, stepping forward and taking the offering from him. I slip my heels off and step onto the blanket, the soft fur slightly cool underneath my feet. Once I'm seated I wrap the other blanket around me and watch as Cole follows suit and removes his shoes then sits directly across from me.

My heart is pounding like a bass drum in my chest and each beat reverberates against my sternum.

"I'm not even sure where to start."

"The truth would be a good spot."

A crease forms on his forehead. I can tell this isn't easy for him, but I won't allow myself to care. I refuse to.

He picks at the blanket for a moment before he draws in a breath and begins. "Back in college I became friends with a guy named Stefan. We met at a frat party and hit it off. Mostly because he wasn't a pompous asshole like a lot of the other kids there who'd grown up with a silver spoon in their mouth—myself included. His dad was in finance on Wall Street and when Stefan graduated he came into some of his trust fund. Rather than follow in his father's footsteps he decided he wanted to do something good with the money."

He glances up at me from where he was looking down at the blanket to see if I'm following along.

Which I'm not.

I mean, I understand everything he's saying, I just have no idea where he's going with this. Regardless, I nod for him to continue.

"Stefan moved to Florida and started up a shelter for battered women. Since college he's been helping women leave abusive relationships and resettle into a new life. Part of the process is giving these women a fresh start. To do that he relies on myself and a few other college buddies to provide them with a job and help settle them in a new city far away from the reach of their abusers."

My mind runs over all the women I've met at Cole's various businesses and I wonder which of them fall into the category of victim.

"That's what Chase was talking about when he threatened to tell your dad about the women . . ." I'd meant only to think it, but before I can stop myself the words are flying out of my mouth.

Cole nods. "Chase overheard a conversation I had with Stefan on the phone one day and put two and two together. He's threatened a few times to expose my secret to my dad. He has no idea and if you knew my dad you'd know that he wouldn't want anything to do with it. My dad's the kind of guy who throws money or a charitable donation at a problem. He's not an in-the-trenches guy."

A few things that have bothered me since our break-up click into place. "That phone call you took that day when you had to leave abruptly . . ."

"One of the women was scared. She thought she heard someone out back of her place. It was nothing, but it took me a while to calm her down."

My shoulders hunch as a little of my indignation leaves my body. My biggest issue was Cole not telling me what Chase was up to, but I'd be lying if I pretended that the little incidents with the women hadn't bothered me. I'd wondered more than a few times whether something had happened with Cole and someone else when we were together.

I pull the blanket tighter around myself. "Why didn't you just tell me?"

"I couldn't break their trust. They're here to leave the past behind them. Not only is it not my story to tell, but if you knew you'd no doubt look at them differently and they wouldn't want that."

I guess that makes sense. "That still doesn't change the fact that you lied to me about Chase. You knew my best friend's fiancé was cheating on her and you didn't say anything." My tone grows heated.

"Whit, I couldn't tell you. Chase was threatening to out me to my dad, which would've meant all these women might lose the jobs that are keeping them afloat. My dad legally owns all those businesses I gave them jobs at. Not only that, but a new woman was coming the next week and if Chase had exposed me she would've had nowhere to go."

"So what? You were planning to stand beside your brother as his best man while you knew he was screwing around?" I'm angrier now.

"No!" He scoots forward and grips my shoulders over the top of the blanket. "I was trying to get him to do the right thing and tell Tahlia what had happened. That's why he barged in that night, because we'd just had it out and I told him he had until the end of the week."

I don't know what to think. Sincerity and frustration are written all over his face. But I'm not sure I can get past the fact that he knowingly lied to me. Over and over again.

"Cole, I think what you're doing for those women is honorable and I understand why you didn't want to tell me . . . wait. Why are you able to tell me now?"

"I spoke to everyone involved, told them what happened and they all agreed that it was okay if I confided in you. I think they've watched me mope around and be miserable for the past month and they're sick of it."

A small laugh escapes me, much to my own annoyance.

"There were so many times I wanted to tell you . . . I just . . . it wasn't just about me or me and you. If it were I would have been honest with you from the start." He leans in and kisses my forehead. I don't pull away. I can't. Once again, I've made

Cole out to be some type of monster in my mind when he's not.

When will I learn? When will I trust someone and stick around to give them the chance to prove themselves in good *and* bad times?

I exhale and feel like I'm releasing all the toxic emotions I've bottled up since I disposed of the man in front of me.

He pulls back and searches my face. The blanket falls from my shoulders and I wrap my arms around his neck.

He pulls me closer so that I'm sitting on his lap.

"I know you don't have any siblings, Whit, but he's my brother. I felt loyal to you *and* to him. We may not be the closest, but I wanted to believe that he'd do the right thing—eventually. I know he loves Tahlia. I thought maybe . . . maybe he just had cold feet about the wedding and would sort his shit out. Chase has always been a little pompous and self-entitled, but it's hard to accept that he's the kind of person who would willingly hurt the woman he asked to marry him."

Cole's right. I don't have a sibling, but I do know what it's like to come to the realization that a member of your family may not be the type of person you expect them to be. I had to come to grips with the fact that both of my own parents didn't want me.

"There's something else you need to know."

His voice is low and serious. It makes my entire body tense, waiting to hear what he says next.

"I want you looking at me when I say this." He pushes my shoulders back and cups my face. "Sweetheart, I am so in love with you. It's been hell without you and I don't want to do it anymore. I need you in my life and I'm not going to take no for an answer. You may not forgive today, or even tomorrow. But I'll be here waiting for you the moment that you do."

He leans forward and places his lips on mine and I open to him immediately. Nothing has ever felt so right as when this man kisses me. Our slow and sensual kiss turns heated right away and before I know it I've shifted myself on his lap so that I'm straddling him.

His hard cock pushes into me from below and I'd give anything right now to get rid of all the fabric between the two of us. I grind down on top of him, anxious for any friction I can get—desperate having missed this so much.

"I can't be without you anymore, Whit." He trails his lips down my throat and his hands reach for the hem of my shirt and in one fluid yank it's up and over my head.

"I can't either. Even when I was mad at you I still loved you."

He stills below me and pulls back to pin me with an intense stare. "You feel the same?" he asks in almost a whisper.

I bite my bottom lip and nod, the corner of my mouth creeping up.

A slow grin transforms his face and I'm not sure I've ever seen him look so happy. "You realize that I'm never letting you go. No matter what bonehead move I make in the future, you're still mine. You'll always be mine."

I reach behind and unclasp my bra. "I think I can live with that." I let the straps fall down my arms and toss it to the side.

His hands cup and knead my breasts. "Good, because you have no choice in the matter." He lowers his head and sucks my nipple into his mouth, teasing it with his tongue and biting down lightly.

"Please don't make me wait any longer," I beg. "I need you inside me."

He doesn't answer, but he does push up and gently lay me on my back so that he hovers over me.

Cole undresses me slowly, trailing kisses over every inch of skin he exposes, and then undresses himself. I take in the way the moonlight bounces off his skin and shadows his muscles while he works away, and I can't believe that this man is mine.

That we are in love with each other.

Six months ago, I was in one of the darkest spots of my life until Cole shone his light on me. The feeling inside me is overwhelming joy and I know that anything is possible.

"In some ways, I'm glad we didn't get that date all those years ago," I say as I pull my head up to meet his lips. "If I'd met you back then I'm not sure we would've made it to here. I wasn't ready for you." He gives me a slow kiss that heats every inch of my exposed skin. "I'm ready now. I am *so* ready."

He slides into me and I know with all my heart and my head that this is what real love feels like. The joining of bodies . . . the joining of lives . . . the joining of hearts. It doesn't mean everything will always be perfect, but it does mean that when things are imperfect you can trust the other person to get you through. I have a partner now and I fully accept and believe that I don't have to do it all on my own anymore.

As I cry out in ecstasy under the full moon and a spattering of stars, I know that I will never stop loving this man—his unicorn cock is just a bonus.

*six months later*

# EPILOGUE

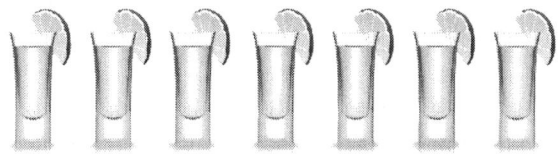

"YOU SURE COME WITH a lot of stuff."

I place the box I'm holding on the kitchen counter and cock a hip. "You love it."

Cole sets my box of shoes down on the floor and steps over to me, drawing me into his body. "I love *you*. I can't say that I love the five thousand pairs of shoes you've brought with you."

"That's a bit of an exaggeration, don't you think?"

He looks behind him at the box he just set down and then to the one set at the entrance to the kitchen and turns his attention back to me. "I'm not so sure about that."

I smack his chest. "Well, if you didn't want all my stuff here you shouldn't have asked me to move in with you."

Cole dips his head and his lips meet mine. In seconds, he deepens the kiss and slides his tongue along the seam of my mouth. I open to allow him entrance and our tongues meet and before I know it our hands are exploring one another's body. My t-shirt is whipped up over my head and tossed somewhere on the floor in a flash.

I come to my senses and pull away, taking a few steps back

from him. "Wait. We can't do this right now. We still have boxes in the U-Haul and it's due back in a couple of hours."

His hungry eyes roam over my body and eventually meet my gaze. "Sweetheart, do you really expect me to look at you standing in front of me like that and *not* do something about it?"

I bite my bottom lip and moan a little because it's so hard to say no to him when he's looking at me like I'm his lunch. But I have no choice. We need to finish hauling everything up here and then Lennon and I have plans to go to Tahlia's and finally drag her back into the land of the living.

"What if we negotiate?" I offer.

He takes one step closer to me. "I'm listening."

"What if we finish getting everything up here, return the truck, and then I give you one of those blow jobs you like so much? Afterwards we can shower together to save time."

Cole doesn't even bother to answer me. Instead he bends down and scoops my shirt up and then pulls it over my head, dressing me as if I'm a child.

"You always have the best ideas." He gives me a chaste kiss and then turns to get back to work.

I laugh and grab a glass from the cupboard, suddenly parched.

"Um . . ."

"What is it?" Once the glass is gripped in my hand I turn around to face him and see exactly what it is. "Sparky! Bad dog!"

The little mutt has dragged one of my shoes out of the box on the floor and is doing his best to turn it into a chew toy.

"Stop it." I spring forward to try to save my shoe, but Sparky just grips it between his teeth and takes off for the living room, wedging himself between the back of the couch and the wall.

It's moments like these that make me question why I decided to be the one to adopt him.

"Those were one of my favorite pairs," I complain.

I hear Cole's footsteps behind me and he takes my hand and leads me out the door. "I'll buy you another pair. Hell, I'll buy you ten. Let's just finish this job because now all I can think about is that blow job, my cock is hard and I'm going to be uncomfortable until your lips are wrapped around me. So, come." He claps his hands in front of him twice. "Chop, chop."

I laugh and get back to work. Truth is, I'm looking forward to it as much as he is.

After a few drinks at Tahlia's house, Lennon and I put our plan to find Tahlia a rebound guy into action. A cab drops us off outside the city's core where a giant white tent is set up with a large temporary fence around the entire area.

"What is this?" Tahlia asks as I pay the taxi driver. She opens her door to exit.

"Excitement, that's what." When they've both exited the back seat, Lennon shuts the door to the taxi and it speeds off.

I pull out my phone and text Cole to let him know we're here.

Lennon doesn't even wait for us and starts heading toward the action, unconcerned as to whether we're following.

I tuck my phone into my back pocket. "Cole's waiting at the gate for us."

"What is this?" Tahl asks again, glancing down at her outfit, no doubt wondering whether she's dressed appropriately. Twenty-something years of upbringing are hard to break.

"It's an amateur boxing fight night. Cole comes here with his friends on occasion."

Tahlia tenses, every muscle in her body appearing rigid.

"Not Chase," I assure her and swing my arm around her shoulders, pulling her into me. "Cole understands that Chase is never to be around me."

"What about when you get married?"

I draw back so she can see me and know I'm not just giving

her lip service. "We'll elope, or forget to mail his invitation."

"It's his brother." She looks doubtful. She clearly doesn't know my blow job skills and my ability to leverage them to get what I want from my man.

"Tahl." I pause until she's looking at me. "Let's not talk about Chase for one night."

A small smile creeps onto her face. "Deal."

I unhook my arm from around her shoulders and we hurry to try to catch Lennon, ready for the fun to begin.

Now, if I'd had *any* idea what was going to go down that night I might never have brought her in the first place.


*The End*

# A note to READERS . . .

What's up Unicorns?

We had a blast writing this together and we hope you had just as much fun reading it!

The person we most want to thank is YOU! That's right! YOU who is reading this right now. Thank you for giving us a chance. We're not new to this whole author thing, but you have no idea who we are and you still chose to give our first book as a writing duo a shot. So, thank you! Whether you loved or hated it, thank you for giving it a chance.

We're not trying to change the world with our work. All we wanted was to create a story that would provide you a few hours entertainment, a bunch of laughs, and hopefully get you squirming in your seat when the characters were having sexy times. If we accomplished that we'll call it a win on our part!

This is the part where we beg you to leave an honest review. Unlike in the bedroom, size *doesn't* matter. Short or long, positive or negative or maybe somewhere in the middle. They all help an author to find the right audience for their book. We'd be super duper grateful if you took two minutes to submit a review to the retailer's site.

If you're on Facebook we hope you'll join us in our reader group—Piper Rayne's Unicorns! Lots of fun, contests, and exclusive giveaways to be had! Oh and man candy. Lots and lots of man candy.

Until next time . . .

XOXO,

Piper & Rayne

P.S.—Don't forget to grab your free copy of the prequel to this story, The Brush-Off and see exactly how Whitney found herself back in San Francisco, falling for the man she swore to hate. Just head to our website at PiperRayne.com and sign-up for our newsletter and it's yours!

# *about*
# PIPER RAYNE

*P*IPER RAYNE, OR PIPER and Rayne, whichever you prefer because we're not one author, we're two. Yep, you get two USA Today Bestselling authors for the price of one. You might be wondering if you know us? Maybe you'll read our books and figure it out. Maybe you won't. Does it really matter?

We aren't trying to stamp ourselves with a top-secret label. We wanted to write without apology. We wanted to not be pigeon-holed into a specific type of story. Everyone has their favorite authors, right? And when you pick up their books, you expect something from them. Whether it's an alpha male, heavy angst, a happily ever after, there's something you are absolutely certain the book will contain. Heck, we're readers, too, we get it!

All that, AND we thought it'd be a helluva lot more fun if we did this writing thing together!

What can we tell you about ourselves? We both have kindle's full of one-clickable books. We're both married to husbands who drive us to drink. We're both chauffeurs to our kids. Most of all, we love hot heroes, quirky heroines that make us laugh, and lots of sexy times. Here's hoping you did, too!

### WE'D LOVE IT IF YOU'D STALK US :

Facebook Page—facebook.com/PiperRayne
Reader Group—facebook.com/groups/PiperRaynesUnicorns
Instagram—authorpiperrayne
Twitter—@piperraynerocks

# other books by
# PIPER RAYNE

Made in the USA
Middletown, DE
14 February 2018